"Someone killed my father." I got out, the words sounding harsh and bald in that quiet room. "I want revenge. He's a witch. I want to strip his powers away."

Suddenly this all seemed so impossible, so unbelievable. What was I doing? Who was I? This wasn't even *me*.

"You believe in witches, then?"

"I have to. I am one."

The woman walked slowly through the shop, as though thinking things over. Every once in a while I felt her dark eyes on me.

"A spell that would strip his powers away is dark magick." You'll bear a mark on your soul forever."

"He killed my father." I felt like tears were not far away.

"I will teach you a spell," the woman said. "If you are truly determined to do this. It won't be easy. Are you prepared for pain? For fear? For darkness?"

His or mine? "Yes," I said, quaking.

"You will need these supplies. Come back when you have them."

A slip of thick gray paper seemed to materialize out of the air.

I took it, my hand shaking. "Okay," I barely whispered.

"Go home, little girl," she said. "Do not come back until you're ready."

By Cate Tiernan

BALEFIRE

SWEEP

BALEFIRE

BOOK FOUR

A NECKLACE OF WATER

CATE TIERNAN

razOr
bill

Balefire 4: A Necklace of Water

RAZORBILL

Published by the Penguin Group
Penguin Young Readers Group
345 Hudson Street, New York, New York 10014, U.S.A.
Penguin Group (USA) Inc., 375 Hudson Street, New York, New York 10014, U.S.A.
Penguin Group (Canada), 90 Eglinton Avenue, Suite 700, Toronto,
Ontario, Canada M4P 2Y3 (a division of Pearson Penguin Canada Inc.)
Penguin Books Ltd, 80 Strand, London WC2R 0RL, England
Penguin Ireland, 25 St Stephen's Green, Dublin 2, Ireland
(a division of Penguin Books Ltd)
Penguin Group (Australia), 250 Camberwell Road, Camberwell,
Victoria 3124, Australia (a division of Pearson Australia Group Pty Ltd)
Penguin Books India Pvt Ltd, 11 Community Centre, Panchsheel Park,
New Delhi - 110 017, India
Penguin Group (NZ), Cnr Airborne and Rosedale Roads, Albany,
Auckland 1310, New Zealand (a division of Pearson New Zealand Ltd)
Penguin Books (South Africa) (Pty) Ltd, 24 Sturdee Avenue, Rosebank,
Johannesburg 2196, South Africa

Penguin Books Ltd, Registered Offices: 80 Strand, London WC2R 0RL, England

10 9 8 7 6 5 4 3 2 1

Copyright 2006 © Gabrielle Charbonnet
All rights reserved

Interior design by Christopher Grassi

Library of Congress Cataloging-in-Publication Data is available

Printed in the United States of America

The publisher does not have any control over and does not assume any responsibility
for author or third-party websites or their content.

To my friend Paul, through all the ups and downs.

Thais

Fire. It was creation and destruction at once. It made life possible, yet could so easily snatch it away. It was a beacon in the darkness, warmth in the coldest winter, an eternal symbol of hearth, home, and comfort.

And it could cook steaks.

I glanced beneath the half-moon kettle standing on rusted legs in our backyard. With one hand I felt around the back—

"Where's the switch?"

My sister looked at me pityingly, then struck a match and laid it on top of the small pile of coals. Nothing happened, and she pulled out another match. Then I saw the barest disturbance—a wavering around the edge of a briquette, as if the air itself were bending.

"There," said Clio, pointing. Sure enough, a timid flame was licking a coal, sliding over it like liquid light, and the next minute the other coals wore tiny frills of dancing orange heat.

The sun was sinking rapidly—though it was still daylight saving time, night was coming sooner every day. Now it was twilight, and shadows and shapes in our yard were becoming less distinct.

"Huh," I said, lost in the way the flames consumed the coals. I looked up at Clio, who was as transfixed as I was. "On mine, we just pressed a switch."

"That's 'cause you're a Yankee," she said absently.

I kicked her shin with my bare foot, and she looked up with a faint grin. "The truth hurts," she said. "I understand." She sat down on our back steps and gathered up her long, straight black hair, using a big plastic clip to hold it off her neck. "Whew," she said. "Hot."

I sat next to her, my own straight black hair awkwardly growing out of a hairstyle I hadn't kept up. Back home in Welsford, Connecticut, I'd had it cut in precise layers every seven weeks. Now I hadn't had a trim in months, ever since my father had been killed and I'd been shuttled down here to New Orleans to live with strangers.

Clio and I let out heavy sighs at the exact same time, then met each other's eyes in a wry acknowledgment of our "twin thing."

I focused on the grill, trying to find words that wouldn't set off yet another argument between me and Clio. In the end, all I could come up with was, "Don't do it."

Clio frowned, not looking at me, and my chest tightened.

Ever since we'd taken part in the horrible, failed rite of the Treize two days ago, Clio and I had been

2

locked in a battle of wills, and we were both losing. It had been an incredibly powerful rite, a rite that could have—should have—been deadly, and Clio and I never should have witnessed it, much less participated.

But we had. And during the rite, at the climax of power and magick and energy, each person in the Treize had privately spoken their deepest wishes. Mine had been to know for sure what had happened to my father last summer. One minute he'd been standing in front of an ice cream shop, and the next he'd been under the front wheels of a Crown Victoria.

I'd been in France, on a class tour of Europe. I'd gotten a phone call from Mrs. Thompkins, our next-door neighbor and closest friend. My life had ended with that phone call, and the surreal existence I'd been living since then still seemed like it belonged to someone else most of the time.

I'd needed to know: How could it be a coincidence that Dad had died, I'd come to New Orleans, and that I'd found not only my identical twin sister but also a bizarre web of history and pain that had been going on for almost 250 years?

It wasn't a coincidence. In my vision I'd seen Daedalus performing the spell that had made old Mrs. Beadle have a stroke. I'd seen him magickally guiding her car onto the sidewalk. He'd smacked his hands together right as the car hit my dad. I'd seen him clench his fist as he ended my dad's life from hundreds of miles away.

Now I wanted to kill him.

Which was impossible, what with the immortality and all. Maybe there was some unknown way I could *try* to kill him, but I'd never be able to carry it out despite what he'd done. I wasn't a murderer like he was.

But I was planning to destroy him. I still knew barely anything about the *bonne magie*, my family's traditional religion, although I'd learned that what you put out into the world, you get back threefold. But if breaking Daedalus came back on me threefold, it would be worth it to avenge my father's death and my life being blown apart for Daedalus's dark purpose.

After the rite, when we were more coherent and less sick, I'd told Clio what I'd seen. Clio had never known Dad, but he was her father too. I was sure she'd feel the same way I did. And she *was* angry at Daedalus, but it was hard to grieve for something she'd never had.

I didn't know what spell she'd tossed into the tornado of magickal force that had knocked us all down at the rite. She told me she'd had a vision of herself drowned. Dead. Her skin pale and bloodless, her sightless eyes staring up at a sky black with storm clouds. It was haunting her.

Clio got up and stirred the glowing coals, edges rimmed with fine white ash, and spread them on the bottom of the kettle. She gauged their temperature with her hand, then set the metal grill in place. We'd marinated a steak, and when she dropped it onto the grate, it sizzled and sent up sharp hisses of steam.

Petra, whom Clio had always thought was her grandmother, had been hit hard by the rite. Since then she'd hardly left her bed, and we were both worried about how frail she suddenly seemed. Maybe making her a steak would strengthen her, along with all the healing spells our friend Melysa was doing.

"I'm going to do it," Clio said, her back still to me. Anger bloomed fast inside my chest, like a scarlet carnation.

I opened my mouth to speak, but Clio turned to face me.

"I don't want to die," she said, for the hundredth time. "I saw myself *dead*. Dead *now*, at this age, not older, not as a grown-up."

"You aren't sure that's what the vision meant," I said carefully, keeping reins on my anger.

"Yes, I am!" she snapped, her green eyes flashing in the deepening night. The birthmark on her left cheek, identical to mine on my right, seemed to blaze brighter, like a splash of blood. "I saw myself *dead*, and it wasn't a dream; it was real. It was what's *about* to happen. And I won't die. Not *now*. Why are you so sure what you saw is real, but what I saw isn't? You're not even a witch!"

I jerked back as if slapped. Clio had grown up as a witch, with Petra and her coven. I'd only found out about the Craft a few months ago. Neither of us had passed the rite of ascension, which in the *bonne magie* would make us full members of a coven.

5

Compared to Clio, I was as stupid as a toddler with all the stuff I didn't know. But it was all too clear that I was a witch, as much a witch as any woman in my family, going back hundreds of years. It was clear that I was going to follow that course till the end of my life.

Clio's lips made an angry, hard line, and I knew she regretted saying that.

"All I'm saying," she went on tightly, "is that you seem to think what you saw is more real than what I saw."

"No, I don't," I insisted. But I'd seen details of something that *had* really happened, and *she'd* had a premonition at best. Who knew if it would ever come true? "I just don't see how you could bear to study with someone who killed our *father*."

Which brought us to the crux of it: Clio had seen herself dead, and it had terrified her. Now she was willing to ally herself with my father's murderer in order to cheat death—death that wasn't even certain.

"Daedalus knows the magick behind the rite better than any of them." Clio jabbed a long fork into the steak and turned it over. Blood dripped onto the blazing coals. "He can teach me what I need to know to make sure the rite works the next time."

"So you'll be immortal," I said tonelessly, and Clio shrugged.

And there you have it: Clio wanted immortality; I wanted to destroy the man who had so coldly ended my dad's life. My dad had been forty-one! Daedalus was, like, 270. Who deserved to live more?

"I know you don't want to die," I said, coming to stand next to her. "I don't *want* you to die. And I don't want to die myself. But you *don't* have to study with Daedalus."

"He knows the most; he's the one who got this together," she said stubbornly.

How could she be so *stupid*? How could she be so disloyal to Dad and to me? "How can you do this!" I shouted in frustration, and Clio wheeled on me, looking furious. Her mouth opened to blast me, but in the next second she froze, as if hearing something.

"Luc," she said, frowning. She glanced at the freshly painted back of our house. "Luc—and Richard."

"Here?"

"Yes." Clio picked up my hand, but only to read my watch. Turning, she stabbed the steak with the fork again, sliding it onto the platter. She headed up the steps with it.

I couldn't believe Clio wouldn't change her mind.

Which was why I could never tell her about my plan to destroy Daedalus.

Clio

Thais was really pissing
me off. Of course I hated the fact that our dad was
dead, that I would never know him, that he'd never
known me. If Daedalus had done it, then I would
have it out with him. Someday.

But in the meantime, I myself was going to be
dead *any day*! In my vision, I'd looked exactly the
same as I did now, not even a year older. I'd seen
myself *dead*, drowned, gray, looking almost exactly
like my ancestor Cerise had when she'd died.

Cerise. My jaw tightened as I set the steak platter down on the kitchen table. I heard Nan in the
front room, talking to Luc and Richard. Great. Just
who I needed to see now together with Thais. Luc,
the man we had both loved and, I was guessing,
both still loved, and Richard, another member of the
Treize, Luc's roommate. Someone who set me off
like gasoline on a fire. Someone who had tried to
kill me and Thais. And had then made out with me.

I frowned, trying to get it together, as Thais came
in from the backyard. Our small wooden table was
set for dinner for three. Iced tea had been poured,

baked potatoes were ready, and a dish of sautéed okra sat in the middle of the table.

"Come in," I heard Nan say, and felt footsteps vibrating the floorboards. It was interesting how our house felt when a man entered it. We were three women, our footsteps light, our energy relatively smooth. Our house felt calm and strong around us. But when a man came into it, everything changed. The energy was charged and jagged, their footsteps so much heavier, voices louder—they took up more space than a woman.

"Oh, Clio," said Nan, her voice still weak. "We . . . have visitors."

The way she said it made me look up. She knew that I had felt them arrive. I wondered if she was still furious at Richard or if she'd forgiven him. And she knew that Luc, Richard, Thais, and I had all kinds of tensions between us—though she didn't know the complete picture about any of it. At least, I prayed she didn't.

"Well, dinner's ready," I said shortly, pulling out my chair and sitting down. Nan came into the kitchen, followed by two people I had rolled around with and now kind of hated. I took a big swig of iced tea, wishing it was Jack Daniels.

Then I saw Luc's face and almost spewed tea out my nose. I heard Thais's gasp behind me, and suddenly Nan's odd tone of voice made sense. I gulped, coughing, trying to get tea down before it blew all over the table.

Finally, holding my napkin to my mouth, I managed, "What happened to your face?"

I flicked a glance at Richard's dark eyes. The

expression on his face told me he'd definitely wanted to be here when I saw Luc for the first time.

"Sit down, Luc," Nan murmured, pulling out her chair. Our kitchen is small, our table smaller, big enough for only three people at one time. I looked at Thais, where she was leaning against the stove, her eyes big and startled. She met my eyes and mouthed, "Holy crap," at me, and I nodded.

Luc sat down across from me, looking miserable. Or at least, I thought he seemed miserable—it was actually hard to tell. I mean, it was hard to tell that he was *human*. Luc—one of the hottest, most handsome guys I'd ever seen in my life, with beautiful bones, beautiful dark blue eyes, a beautiful sculpted mouth that I had been unable to resist—now looked like the Thing.

His face was grossly swollen, his features obscured. His eyes seemed small and piggy, almost closed with extra flesh. His skin itself, usually gorgeous, perfect, and tan, was now waxen and pasty, covered with thousands of tiny pustules. Clearly he'd had trouble shaving: several days' worth of dark stubble mottled his cheeks and chin, and not in a sexy way.

He looked like a monster.

"Yep," Richard said, walking to the fridge and helping himself to one of Nan's beers. "I'm guessing someone at the rite wanted everyone's outsides to match their insides."

"Shut up," said Luc, his voice sounding like it had been put through a cheese grater. He sounded very subdued, very different from his usual world-weary, ironic self.

10

Richard grinned and toasted him with the beer, then tilted his head back and drank. I tried to put all images of kissing and biting that neck out of my mind.

"But what happened?" said Thais, sounding appalled. "Did someone do this? Or is this, like, from something you ate or touched? Poison ivy?"

Luc laughed wryly. "No, this is magickal. I don't know why or how or who. Someone wanted to teach me a lesson, I guess."

His gaze flicked past Thais to me, and I frowned. He knew Thais and I had every reason to despise him, but neither of us would ever do anything like this.

Tempting though it would be.

"It wasn't me," I said.

"It wasn't me," Thais echoed.

"It wasn't me," Richard put in. "Though God knows I'm enjoying the hell out of it."

Luc shot him an angry glance, and Richard grinned. It burned Richard up, how I felt about Luc—not that he wanted me himself. Or at least, not for more than twenty minutes at a time.

Nan took Luc's chin in her hand, tilting his face in the red-tinged twilight to see it better. "It would help if we knew who had done this," she murmured, and she suddenly looked so old that I almost drew in my breath. Nan had looked exactly the same for my entire life— seventeen years. Now, two days after the rite, she looked so much paler, weaker. Not as if she'd actually physically aged in any way, but had just . . . been drained.

So many spells had been cast at that rite, so

much changed for all of us. When would we know everything that had been set in motion? What each member of the Treize had used that tremendous assimilation of power to accomplish? I shivered at the thought.

"But I think we can do something, not knowing who it was or what they used," Nan continued. "Skin problems are usually caused by something acting on the liver—the seat of anger or hostility. I would guess some kind of anger recoiled on the liver, and it's pushing a psychoenergetic poison out through your skin from the inside."

Yep, that would have been my first guess too.

Nan looked up at me, her pale blue-gray eyes tired but still bright. "Honey, go into the workroom and get me some broadleaf dock leaves. Plus red clover and vervain. Asabarraca. And there's a jar labeled *French Clay*, if you could bring that, and . . ." She paused, thinking. "I guess that's it—we'll start with that. And Thais, fetch the rosemary and sage out of the pantry. Oh, and the comfrey tea."

"Comfrey tea wrecks your kidneys," I threw over my shoulder as I headed to the workroom.

"You can't drink it for more than three days," Nan reminded me. "Or it will."

I was standing in front of Nan's work cupboard when I felt Richard come up behind me. For one second I felt afraid—I couldn't forget that he'd tried to hurt me and Thais. But I also believed, as Nan did, that he would never do it now.

"Go away," I said, my back to him.

"Come to help you carry," he said in that sardonic voice that always felt like a challenge. "'Cause I'm that kind of guy."

I gave him a narrow-eyed look. "Don't even get me started on what kind of guy you are." I saw his jaw tighten as he tried to keep his temper from flaring. Turning back to Nan's cupboard, I examined small brown glass bottles filled with essences and extracts, dried this and powdered that. I set the asabarraca on the worktable, then found the ceramic jar of French clay. Next I went through files of pressed, dried leaves and flowers, organized not alphabetically but according to what larger family they were from and, within that, to the subcategories of what effects they would cause.

I knew this stuff pretty well and usually could put my hand on what I needed pretty quickly. But having Richard breathing down my neck made me tense, and I forgot what I was looking for.

"Go away," I said again, irritably.

"Look, we have to get this straight between us," he said in a low voice.

"Get what straight? The fact that you tried to kill me and my sister?" Wide-eyed, I cocked my head, looking confused. "Is that what you're talking about? The attempted murder stuff?"

"Yeah, yeah," he said tensely. "My bad. Can we move on from that?"

I gaped at him. "Move *on*? Move on from attem—" I was literally speechless.

He waved his hand impatiently. "I explained all that.

13

That was before I even *knew* you. Just . . . get over it. We need to figure this out, what we have between us."

"We don't have *anything* between us!" I hissed, trying to keep my voice down.

"That's bull, and you know it!" he said, just as angrily. He moved closer to me, and I felt his indescribable force, as if we were literally magnets, positive and negative, irresistibly drawn together whether we wanted to be or not.

I kept my arms at my sides, as stiff as poles. I hated this! Hated what he did to me. "We have *nothing*," I said again, and turned back to the plant file. *Red dock, red dock* . . . My fingers flipped through plastic sleeves, all neatly labeled and dated.

In the next moment he curved his arms around me, pressing his body against my back from shoulder to hip. His arms crossed, holding me tightly, his right hand pulling my hips against him, his left hand curling up to hold my right shoulder.

"Don't say that," he murmured into my hair while all my nerve endings started exploding. I felt his breath warm on my neck, and then he bit me gently, right where my neck curved into my shoulder. I shuddered and my brain shorted out for a moment.

But just for a moment. I brought my arms up hard, breaking his hold, and though he'd trapped me between himself and the cupboard, I wheeled, ready to rip into him.

I didn't have a chance. He lowered his head lightning fast and kissed me, pushing me against the open cupboard so that it teetered on its legs. He

14

pressed hard against me, trying to make as much of me touch as much of him as possible. *Not again.*

His mouth was warm and hard, and I instantly recognized it. My body recognized his; my mouth knew the touch and pressure and taste of his. I could smell the slight smokiness of his clothes and hair and the fresh detergent scent of his shirt. It felt like, *At last.* I started to weaken, like honey warmed by the sun, becoming softer, more fluid.

But because I still somehow had two synapses left to rub together, I broke from his hold again, pushing his chest hard, shoving him. He was breathing fast, chest rising and falling, and his dark, dark eyes looked lit by flames.

"Get off me!" I said too loudly, and lowered my voice. "Get away from me," I whispered furiously. "There's nothing between us; there'll *never* be anything between us! Now get the hell out of my way!"

Staring at me angrily, he held up his hands— surrender. He picked up the jars of French clay and asabarraca and headed toward the kitchen. "Get the rest of the stuff."

Then I was alone in the workroom, feeling like I was losing my mind.

Unfortunately, I knew myself well enough to know that I was partly angry at him and partly angry at myself for wanting him despite everything. He'd set up horrifying accidents for me and Thais; he didn't love me, didn't love anybody. . . .

But something about him caused my body to go into hyperdrive. Something inside me wanted him, wanted desperately to meld with him no matter what he or I rationally wanted or thought. I took some slow, steady breaths, trying to calm myself. I pressed my palms against my cheeks, which felt like they were on fire.

I forced myself to remember what else Nan had said. Thais was getting rosemary and stuff—oh, broadleaf dock leaves. Red clover. All this stuff had purifying, cleansing properties. The vervain would give everything an extra boost.

I brought the vervain and dried leaves back into the kitchen, where the kettle was boiling.

"Thank you, sweetie," Nan said, getting out her mortar and pestle. "There's a small jar in the back of the cupboard marked *Cinders*. Get that too."

I nodded, refusing to look at Richard, who leaned against the fridge, drinking his beer. In moments I came back with the jar of ashes, collected from various sacred fires.

Our food was cold on the table. I had lost my appetite anyway. My hands clenched and unclenched nervously. I had to get out of here. Just being around Richard, much less Richard and Luc together, was making me feel like I was coming out of my skin.

"Okay, Luc," said Nan, sounding a bit more brisk. "Four things. A tea to make and drink one cup of three times a day. I'll write it out for you. It'll help cleanse and strengthen your liver. A wash to use on your skin, also three times a day. A mask to use once a day. You put it on, let it dry, then gently wash it off. And finally, a spell to perform twice

16

a day, at noon and midnight, that will help channel this anger and energy out of you."

"Thank you, Petra," said Luc, his voice muffled. "I really appreciate it." I'd never seen him like this—it was like his gorgeous outer shell had split to reveal this ugly, less cocky version of himself.

Someone had done this to him magickally. Someone pretty strong. One of the Treize.

I wished I'd thought of it.

I still felt burned about what he had done to me and Thais. My heart still felt broken. And in weak moments that I hadn't admitted to anyone, I still wanted him to be mine and only mine. But I had to say—seeing him like this made it a little easier somehow.

"Has anyone else been affected like this?" Thais asked. I'd been avoiding her eyes, not wanting to know if she was watching Luc, but now I looked at her. She seemed stiff and uncomfortable, but whether because of Luc or Richard or our fight, I didn't know.

Luc and Richard glanced at each other, and Luc said, "No, not like this. But Manon has moved out. She's left Sophie. Right now she's staying with Axelle."

"Such a good idea," Richard murmured.

"Why did she move out?" Thais asked.

"It turns out she tried to use the rite to kill herself, like Marcel did," Luc explained. "But without anyone else's help."

Nan shrugged wryly.

"But Sophie worked against her, preventing her spell from taking effect—not that it even would have," Luc went on. "Manon realized it and felt like

17

Sophie had betrayed her. They had a fight, and Manon broke up with her."

"Oh, my goodness," Nan murmured, her hand to her chest.

"Wow," said Thais. "How long had they been together?"

"Uh . . ." Richard thought. "About a hundred and twenty years, I think. Something like that. They have a big fight every forty years or so. This will probably blow over."

"I don't know," said Luc. "This seems different. Manon was . . . more than furious."

"Women!" Richard shook his head, and I gave him an angry glare. He grinned at me and I quickly looked away. When Richard smiled, he looked like an angel who had been kicked out of heaven.

"Daedalus seems to still feel weak from it," Luc said, his eyes on Nan. He must have noticed how she looking, how she was acting.

Nan nodded gravely.

"But no one else has anything like this," Luc said, gesturing to his face in disgust. "This is all mine."

"I think it will improve," Nan said. "It's not permanent. Just follow this regimen and in three weeks you'll be recognizable."

"Three weeks?" Luc sounded horrified.

"You'll be okay," Richard said, patting Luc's shoulder. "It'll be good for you. Character-building. See how the other half lives. Man on the street and so on. Instead of that male-model babe-magnet thing you usually have going."

Thais made a strangled sound, and I had to forcibly swallow a shriek of rage. Luc's babe-magnet effect had broken my heart and Thais's as well. Trust Richard to rub our noses in it.

"I'm going to Racey's," I said abruptly.

"But you haven't eaten," said Nan.

"Not hungry anymore."

"Well, okay," Nan said, "but don't stay out late. It's a school night."

"Okay." I made sure Nan wasn't looking, and then I stuck my tongue out at Richard. His eyebrows shot up and he grinned again. I turned and hightailed it out of the kitchen, but not before I'd glimpsed Thais's startled face—she'd seen me. But she didn't know the whole story between me and Richard, and she never would.

My purse and the keys to our dinky little rental car were by the front door. Outside, it was completely dark, a pleasant, balmy evening, maybe in the sixties. It was October. In a little less than four weeks our most important festival, Monvoile, would take place. It was a time of supreme magick, when the mists between the worlds thinned and pulled back slightly. And I had a plan for it.

I got in the car and started the engine, picturing tired little squirrels pedaling, making the engine run. As I pulled away from the curb, I felt Richard's presence lingering behind me. To hell with him. Jerk. I pulled out my cell phone.

"Race? Listen, if anyone asks, I'm at your house, okay?"

A Hollow Shell Within a Year

Daedalus tilted the shade of his dresser lamp to throw light more directly on his face. Peering into his mirror, he turned one cheek toward it, then the other. Two days after the rite, his eyes were sunken, his forehead furrowed, his lips thinner.

His powers were weakening, and it showed on his face.

He had no idea how this had happened, only when—at the rite. The failed rite that he had planned for, dreamed of, researched for more than two hundred years. It hadn't been the perfect re-creation—no one had been pregnant. Several people had been brought there by force. The actual Source had not been bubbling up from the ground at their feet. Plus the twins, with their power—that could have been enough to throw the whole thing off. Everything that had been under his control—the timing, tools, the spells themselves, the location—all that had been perfect. But he wasn't able to completely control the Treize—not the way Melita had.

And, of course, Petra had actively worked

against him. Petra, Marcel, Ouida, probably others that he wasn't aware of. They'd worked against him, betrayed him. And now look at him—getting weaker every day. He wasn't positive that someone had specifically spelled him to weaken like this or whether it was just an effect of the rite's energy going haywire, being misused. But he would find out.

He had to prevent anyone from realizing what had happened to him. He couldn't afford to look weaker. Now, in front of the mirror, he practiced standing up straighter, holding back his shoulders, trying to firm his jaw.

Depression settled on his shoulders, making them sag. His power was leaking slowly out of him day by day, as if it were sugar trickling from a tiny hole in a sack. At this rate, he would be a hollow shell, a grotesque, powerless, walking skeleton, within a year.

He had no choice now. Melita *must* be found. Then the two of them would do whatever it took to reopen the Source and completely re-perform the rite again in its entirety. With any luck, someone would be pregnant by then. He would have to speak to Luc, find out what was going on with that. If Luc hadn't made such a monumental blunder in the first place—

Anyway. His own path now was clear. But with Melita back, they would no longer be a Treize. One person would be superfluous and would need to be eliminated. One of the twins, to break up their joint power? Or someone whose loyalties were clearly not with him? Or the weakest person?

He would have to decide, and soon, before he lost any more strength.

His doorbell rang, startling him. This problem had so consumed him that he hadn't felt anyone approaching, even coming up the stairs.

He cast his senses and frowned when he realized who it was. What would she want?

Before he opened the apartment door, he squared his shoulders and stood up straight, putting a stern frown on his face to seem stronger.

"Hello, Daedalus." Clio was trying to look casual, but he read tension in her shifting feet, the way one hand held her purse strap so tightly.

Daedalus glanced quickly past her out onto the covered balcony. She was alone.

"Who sent you?" he asked brusquely. "What do you want? I'm very busy."

"I know," said Clio, sounding more sure of herself.

"Well?"

"I want—I want you to teach me." Cerise's beautiful leaf green eyes looked at him out of Clio's face. In a moment, he was transported back 240 years.

"I want to be immortal," she said.

Clio

I waited on Daedalus's doorstep, trying to look brave and calm. "You offered to teach me that night in the cemetery," I reminded him. "I want to take you up on it."

"Petra just worked against me during the most important rite of the last two centuries," Daedalus said coolly. "Does she know you're here?"

I hesitated. If I said no, would he take it as permission to kill me and chop me up into little pieces?

"No," I said, just as coolly, raising my chin. After all, I was Clio Martin, and I'd been making guys—young and old—quake at the knees since I was fourteen. "But Thais does."

In a general way. Not a specific right-now way. And she would have killed me if she did know.

Daedalus looked at me. Lamps cast a soft amber glow over the walls, making the fourteen-foot ceilings look even higher. He seemed to make a decision and stepped back from the door. He gestured me in, and I expected spooky symbolic music to start playing, like "crossing the threshold, ooh."

Like he had the first time we'd all met in his

apartment, Daedalus went to a small table with crystal decanters laid out as though part of a movie set. He poured some plum-colored liquid into two miniature wineglasses and handed me one. It smelled nutty and warm and sweet. I waited for him to drink his first, since I hadn't just fallen off the turnip truck. He took a small sip, seeming to savor it before swallowing.

I decided to wait on mine. Time to get down to business.

"Look," I said, taking a deep breath. "The rite. I don't know what happened with everyone else. But I had a vision. I saw myself dead. Drowned. I don't know why." I walked past him to the tall French windows that led to his balcony overlooking the narrow street. "I don't want to die. Not now, not ever. I want to be immortal, like you and the Treize. Teach me how to do the rite, whatever I need to do, to make it work."

I looked at him, still standing by his drinks tray. What if he had changed his mind?

"I saw myself *dead*," I repeated, trying to keep desperation out of my voice. "It wasn't just a vision—it was real. It's going to happen. I don't know when, but soon. I have to stop it."

I forced myself to wait, looking as calm as I could. I didn't want to give him any more power over me than I had to.

Finally he spoke. "So you want to participate, to help raise the power and channel it, instead of merely watch?"

"Yes."

His eyes narrowed at me, and his glance flicked down to my untried glass of port.

"Who sent you?"

"No one. I want you to teach me. Are you up for it or not? Do you *have* anything you can teach me?" I injected just the faintest tinge of skepticism into my voice, figuring that his Y-chromosome bullheadedness would kick in.

It did.

"I've forgotten more about magick than you'll ever learn," he said, anger flushing his hollow cheeks.

I paused and took a sip of the wine. It left a trail of heat down my throat and into my stomach. I *so* hoped I hadn't just done something stupid. "How pithy," I said, watching him casually, as if he were a science experiment. "Did you make that up?"

His jaw set, and the way the light hit him just then made me realize that he looked frailer today than he had before the rite. Like Nan. Was he losing some of his power too? Then Daedalus seemed to get ahold of his anger, and he relaxed.

He smiled. "You're tough, aren't you, Clio?"

I stood there and tried to send out "tough" vibes.

"How tough, I wonder?" Daedalus said, almost to himself, and walked toward me.

I am immovable, I thought. *I am a rock.*

When he was close enough, he reached out one hand and gently placed three fingers at my temple. Too late I realized what he might do and jerked away, but he grabbed my arm tightly with his other hand and held me in place.

25

I closed my eyes, panicking, trying to shut my brain down, shut everything—

But it was too late, and he was too strong. In moments he had gained access into my consciousness, and then things became blurred. Second by second, I received lightning-fast patchwork impressions of a thousand different memories, over and over—for how long, I don't know. Memories of my childhood, my first kiss, my first spell, being afraid, nightmares, being sick, feeling triumphant—a thousand pictures and emotions flashed inside my head like a film speeded up to incomprehensibility. I felt terrified, on a roller coaster of emotions from hell, and wished desperately that I hadn't come. I had to get out of here, had to escape, had to—and then Daedalus turned me loose. I staggered and almost fell.

I caught myself on the back of a wingback chair, seizing the tapestry, rough under my fingers, and held on. I was breathing hard and felt like he had poured Drano on my brain and then caught my rushing memories in a steel basin. My other hand was curled into a claw, and I realized with amazement that I hadn't dropped the port glass. Slowly, slowly I came back to myself, trying to contain my consciousness, to pin my fear beneath my heel. When I could, I raised my eyes and looked at Daedalus, unsure how much time had passed, what he had seen, how he had done it. I'd heard of people doing this, witches, and Thais and I together had done a mutual version of it to become closer. But I hadn't realized that someone could do it so easily, at a moment's notice. He really was much stronger than I'd realized. I was in over my head.

No, I wasn't. I could do this. *I* was stronger than I realized.

I stood up straight, trying too late to look unaffected, to control my breathing, and took another little sip of port. It felt like drinking blood, warm, rich, heating my veins and filling me with life.

Suddenly I wondered if it was spelled. *Oops.* What the hell was I doing? If Thais was right about him, then I was being about as stupid as I could possibly be. But if she was wrong—

Daedalus was standing several feet away, watching me.

I tilted my chin a little, as if issuing a dare, pretending I wasn't terrified that he might have just wiped my brain clean of all memories.

No. I knew I was Clio. I had a sister. We lived with our twelve-greats-in-a-row grandmother.

"You do want to learn," he said.

"Yes." My brain understood his words. Oh, thank God.

"You came on your own."

"Yes."

"Thais doesn't know. She thinks you're at Racey's."

Crap.

Would I survive if I threw myself out the window and over the balcony to the street below? How high was it? Eighteen feet?

27

Suddenly Daedalus turned away, all business. He put down his glass and smoothed his goatee in the empire mirror over the table. "Well, come here. Let's see what you make of this."

I followed him into his formal dining room, which had paneling below the chair rail and old-fashioned flowered wallpaper above. As in Axelle's apartment, a heavy molding had been used for the chair rail, and more edged the high ceiling. Daedalus paused by a section of the wall and lightly drew his fingers across the wallpaper, whispering things I couldn't hear.

I heard the faintest click, and then a small door-way, invisible before now, opened inward. Thais had told me about something almost exactly the same that Axelle had in her apartment. Did every witch have something like this? Just the Treize? Did Nan have one somewhere that I'd never found?

The interior of the space was dark. Daedalus picked up a four-armed silver candelabra and brushed his fingers over the candlewicks. They ignited instantly, and I thought, *So effing cool.* He went inside, gesturing to me to follow him.

In a movie, this would be the part where the audience is screaming, "Don't go in!" And then of course the stupid heroine goes in, and then the ax murderer gets her. I stepped in, my heart beating in my throat, hoping there would be enough left of me to identify the body.

We were standing in a space about five feet wide and maybe seven feet long. The interior was painted black, making the space seem smaller. Everywhere were painted silver symbols, making borders along each edge, covering the walls. I saw a cornucopia spilling tears of blood that made me shudder, though I tried to hide it. There were words in Old French, most of which I knew. And of course there were runes—all the usual ones I recognized, and then some I didn't. I tried to have no reaction when I saw the same symbols here that I'd seen on Richard's walls, in his room at Luc's apartment.

Come to think of it, there were a lot of similarities. Both had used silver paint on a dark background; both had these ubfamiliar symbols. What did that mean?

Black candles in small silver holders were everywhere, some new, some guttered. I looked down to see if they had dripped onto the floor and saw that the floor was also painted black, and a large silver-painted pentacle almost touched all four walls. For a minute I just looked around, hoping I wouldn't see a shrunken head or a jar of newt eyes. And I'm a *witch*.

"How do you think immortality works, Clio?" Daedalus asked. On a narrow ledge, a large leather-bound book lay open.

"The Source," I said, looking at him. "It was, like, the fountain of youth or something."

"I'm not sure what the Source is," he said, setting his candelabra on a very small, narrow table. He flipped through the yellowed, deckle-edged pages of his book. "I think it's a power enhancer, whether it's

29

a life force or magickal power, nature, growing things."

"But it by itself isn't a fountain of youth?"

"It might be," Daedalus said. "But I don't think so. I think it just lent us power to prolong our lives. And I think we need to find it again if we're going to lend immortality to anyone else. But we can still accomplish a great deal without it. I can teach you how to get power from other things, and then, when we find the Source, you'll be ready."

That sounded like what I wanted. "What other things?" I pictured small dead animals and knew I just couldn't do anything like that.

Daedalus looked at me, his blue eyes glittering. "Almost anything," he said, his voice mild. "From fire, from water, from plants, from the ground itself. From animals. From people."

I had a split-second image of Cerise, dead on the ground, followed immediately by an image of myself, also dead on the ground. Drowned. Was that what was going to happen to me? Would someone kill me to use my power? It wouldn't make sense—there were so many people who were stronger than me and whose power would be more useful.

But those people were immortal.

Oh.

"I see," I said, nodding. I had wondered whether to tell him about the awful, wonderful spell I had done on the neighborhood cats and decided not to. I didn't want him to think I was more evil than I actually was. I mean, I'm totally not evil at all, but telling him about that spell might give him the wrong impression.

"I'm not sure you do see," Daedalus said, "but I can show you. Let me walk you through a simple spell, teach you how to take something's power."

"You mean subvert its power?" Which was what I had done to the cats. Borrowed their power.

"No. Actually take its power. To keep."

Please, Deésse, don't let him bring out a live animal, I prayed, feeling my stomach tighten.

Instead he opened a wooden box, painted black and inset with a silver *D*, which seemed kind of prosaic—like, it should have been another pentacle or a rune or some other symbol instead of just his initial. He took out an egg-size chunk of smoky quartz, uncut, just an irregular, flawed hunk of crystal.

"Everything has energy, Clio," he said softly, holding out the crystal. "Everything is vibrating, according to its nature. If you attune your vibrations, you can assume them. Then it will become part of you, and its power will be yours to use."

A tingle of excitement stirred despite my nervousness and tension. I licked my lips, looking at the crystal.

"How do we do it?" I asked.

"*Ce n'est pas facile,*" he said, unexpectedly switching to French.

"*Oui, comprends,*" I said.

He gave a quick nod, then gestured to my purse, which I was clutching as though it were a lifeline.

31

"Put that down and any electronic things you might have, like a phone or digital watch or a—what do you call it—a pager."

I set my purse outside the door of the little secret room, fully aware that my cell phone was in it and that without it I was completely alone and unreachable. Daedalus waved his hand in the air and the small door silently swung shut. I could just barely make out its outline in the black wall, and I thought, *Oh, frick.* My heart started pounding so hard I wondered if Daedalus could hear it.

My whole life I'd lived with a witch, Nan, and around witches. Nan had always been much, much stronger than anyone else. I had been the second strongest. Now I knew it was because of our heritage, because of the Treize. Even so, I'd never seen Nan just wave her hand and close a door. *She'd probably think it was tacky,* I thought with rising hysteria.

I looked up at Daedalus, at his cold, unreadable eyes. He looked very intent, focused on me, and I hoped it was because he was glad to have someone who wanted to learn.

"Come," he said, holding out his hand, and I stepped closer to the exact center of the silver pentacle on the floor. A long, slim black wand was resting on a shelf, and he took it and traced the pentacle's circumference with it. Our circle was cast. Then he placed my right hand over the crystal in his hand so that we were holding it together.

"First we center ourselves where we are and get in touch with our own power," he said softly. I'd never been this close to him before, and I was uncomfortable and unbearably tense. Suddenly I was afraid that I wouldn't be able to concentrate, that I would choke and look weak in front of him. I had to show him that I was strong, that I could do this.

Clio, do not screw this up. It felt like my whole future was in this moment, that whether I would live or die, literally, depended on the outcome of this situation.

I shut my mouth and breathed out slowly through my nose. Consciously I released all fear and regrets, just let them go and agreed to accept whatever happened.

Which, of course, is always the first step to getting in touch with magick.

"The first part of this spell binds us to the earth," Daedalus said. "Even though we're on the second floor."

His eyes twinkled. I'd never seen any sense of humor about him before, and it made him seem a bit less scary—a tiny bit.

"The second part recognizes the crystal's vibrations," he went on in a soft, soothing voice. "And the third part aligns our vibrations with its. Can you tell me what the fourth part of the spell would be? The *fin-quatrième?*"

Spells were divided up into parts, sometimes as many as twelve or thirteen, depending on what you were doing. I knew that spells with even more parts or steps than that existed, but I'd never done any of them, never seen them done. Putting the prefix *fin-* in front of *quatrième* meant that the spell had only four parts and that the fourth part was the last.

"The *fin-quatrième* would be taking its power," I said. I had no problem with taking a crystal's power. It didn't seem alive, couldn't feel pain or fear. This was fine.

Daedalus started teaching me the spell. I knew the basic form, the grounding and centering, and I copied it perfectly. He seemed pleased, and I started to feel better.

The second part was also familiar—anytime you use anything whatsoever in a spell, you have to recognize it, learn it, identify it. The third part was a variation on what I had done that night with the cats, but it seemed less scary and dangerous. I concentrated hard, memorizing it, and almost gasped when I felt my vibrations subtly align with the crystal's. My eyes were closed and I was breathing shallowly through my mouth. I felt the crystal practically burning between our hands—Daedalus and I seemed like one, and then we joined the crystal and it was like we were no longer two beings, Clio and Daedalus, but one new, alien life-form made up of our two vibrations plus this other, weird vibration of the crystal. You couldn't picture it in your mind, and I can't describe it. But that was what it felt like.

Then Daedalus started singing the *fin-quatrième*. I paid intense attention, though since we were linked, the words weren't even words—they were images and emotions and meanings, and they went straight into my brain from his, and I started singing them too, though I'd never heard them before. It was a beautiful spell, elegant and precise, sparely written, with no extraneous showmanship or clumsy, unnecessary elements. It was actually a much better spell than I would have thought Daedalus might craft—but then again, maybe he hadn't crafted it.

Suddenly the tone changed. I was in the middle of admiring the spell, memorizing it even as I sang it for the first time, and then it was as if the world went dark. I didn't open my eyes, but a heavy gray veil suddenly seemed to drop down over everything, separating me and Daedalus and the crystal from the rest of the world. A tendril of fear uncoiled at the base of my spine, but I ignored it, concentrating on the spell.

The spell started to unravel the crystal, separating its vibrations and energy from its form. It wasn't a clean break; it wasn't as if you could simply assume its power and still be left with a whole crystal. With horror I realized that the only way to get power from something was to destroy it utterly. The vibrations were being dismantled, untwined from their hold on the crystal's perfect, beautiful structure of neatly aligned atoms. Like a storm pulling a rosebush off a trellis, the spell slowly ripped away the crystal's energy. It was devastating. Then I was almost thrown backward as a sharp, clear burst of energy jolted into me, spearing my chest and filling me with light and fire.

My eyes popped open to stare into the glittering

blue eyes of an ancient witch. His face was alight, younger, his cheeks flushed and not so sunken. An insane riptide of joy submerged me as I felt the huge, spiraling power within me, far more powerful than anything I'd felt before, either at a circle or with the cats. I felt like I was glowing in the dark, that I could walk down the street and bring trees back to life, heal children, wave my hand and solve any problem.

Daedalus smiled at the look on my face. I realized his hands were holding mine firmly, which was why I hadn't been knocked out of the circle when the crystal's energy entered me.

"Do you see, Clio?" His lips didn't move, but I heard the words clearly. "Do you see how something's power can become yours for the taking? Do you see what life can feel like?"

I nodded, speechless, my head buzzing with wonder, my knees shaking. If I opened my mouth to speak, white light would pour out, lighting this black room like sunlight at noon.

I was ecstatic, intensely happy, filled with light and love and power beyond all comprehension. It was the most incredible feeling I could possibly imagine—I'd had no idea such a thing was possible, and in one second I knew that I wanted it, needed it, had to have it all the time. *What now*, I thought eagerly—*do we do another spell to keep it with us? How long will this last? Can I add to this?*

With no warning, I felt it start to drain away.

Alarmed, I looked into Daedalus's eyes and saw

my knowledge confirmed there. He knew it was already fading.

"No, no," I whispered. "Don't let it go!"

He shook his head, and we continued to breathe slowly in and out in unison. The power leached out of me, like bones being bleached in the sun. I wanted to cry as I felt it leave me, felt my joy and passion and power and strength fade, leaving me diminished, heartbroken, a pale reflection of the glorious creature I had been only minutes earlier.

I felt utterly shattered, as if my bones were turning to lace. My right hand clenched the crystal like a frozen claw, and with difficulty I unpeeled my fingers.

Where the chunk of smoky quartz had been, there was now only a pile of ashy white powder. As soon as I took my hand away, it began to sift through Daedalus's shaking hand.

Abruptly my legs gave way and I fell to the floor.

Effortless, Like Melita

It was amazing, Axelle thought. Her black eyes focused unwaveringly on the black candle, hovering an inch over her black marble countertop. Her thought was a nebulous ribbon fluttering at the edge of her brain while most of her consciousness spun magick.

Axelle had never been able to levitate a candle, even after Melita had increased their powers, after Axelle had been studying magick, off and on, for almost two hundred years.

Now look at her.

It felt effortless, a smooth extension of herself, as if her will extended beyond the boundaries of her person to affect the world around her without even touching it.

This was all new since the failed rite. During the rite she had asked for more power. She had gotten it. And this newfound power was intoxicating. She knew that all of magick was balance—that if she had gained power, someone had lost it. But truly, why should she care?

"Mrew?" Minou jumped up on the counter next

to the hovering candle. Her pupils flared when she sensed the magickal field, and when she saw the candle, she batted at it.

Axelle blinked, the candle fell, and the spell was broken. Minou's tail puffed instantly, and she jumped off the counter to hide under the couch. The whole thing had taken two seconds.

Nearby, Manon managed half a smile, which was the most Axelle had seen since Manon had shown up on her doorstep, suitcase in hand. Yeah, Sophie had screwed up big this time. Not that Manon's plan would have worked anyway—look at what Marcel had gone through. Axelle sighed. Marcel. When was he going to get tired of being a little storm cloud, raining on everyone's parade? Goddess knew *she* was tired of it.

But Sophie had blocked Manon's plan, when if she had just sat tight and not done anything, it would have ended up the way she wanted. Now Manon felt betrayed, like Sophie had stabbed her in the back. Which, as they all knew, wouldn't have helped her plan either.

"You couldn't do that before, could you?" Manon asked.

"No," said Axelle, picking up the candle. "I'm stronger since the rite." She looked up at Manon, used to her childish face and body, the blond hair, the dark eyes so oddly old and jaded and bitter in that pretty, girlish face. "You know, this is what Melita feels like all the time. Better than this. Stronger than this." Axelle looked down at her

39

perfectly manicured hands, the slim fingers that now seemed able to command magick at will.

"I never really realized it before," Axelle went on. "We all knew she was wicked strong, but I never understood what that meant. It meant this." She twined her white hands in the air, not making magick, but moving them slowly and gracefully through space. "It felt like part of her, easy and natural. I mean, I think things, and they come to me. It always seemed to take so much effort before. Studying books, memorizing things, practicing forms again and again. This is the difference between taking endless years of violin lessons and being born a virtuoso."

Manon looked at her. "Do you feel like a virtuoso now, with magick?"

Axelle thought. "It's just . . . so much easier. It comes to me. Before, I had to hunt magick down, wrest it out of the world, force it to my will. Now it feels there, everywhere, accessible. I can pluck it out of the air like a kite string." She made a pinching motion with one hand. "It's smooth."

"That's amazing." Manon sounded bitter—she hadn't gotten what she'd asked for from the rite. Her brown eyes looked bruised from crying, her small face pinched and pale. Axelle still had no idea what Manon saw in Sophie—Sophie seemed so staid, so boring and prissy and goody-goody. Not that Manon was that bent. But she could have done so much better. If Axelle had been Manon, had been made immortal as a beautiful child, she would have found a way to turn it to her advantage instead of whining about it for a quarter of a millennium.

"The thing is," Axelle said, going to the fridge and taking the bottle of vodka out of the freezer, "this is what Melita felt back then. And who knows what she's got now, what kind of power? But back then, she had this, possibly more, and she kept it to herself."

"What do you mean? She showed us all the Source; she did the rite," said Manon.

Axelle poured herself three fingers of vodka in a glass she hoped was clean. Manon wasn't the little homemaker Thais had been, and the place was a wreck. "But she didn't truly share her power. Yeah, she did the rite, made us all immortal, yippee. But only because she wanted immortality for herself as well. Before then she was this strong for, what, ten years? A long time. And she didn't share that, didn't tell anyone else how to get it."

Manon frowned, then picked up her glass and went into the big main room. She sank down on a black leather chair with her back against one arm and her legs dangling over the other. "Well, why would she? People who have power want to keep it for themselves."

"You don't understand." Axelle lay down on the couch, her clothes sliding against the leather. She punched a pillow into place so her head was still high enough for her to drink. "I was Melita's best friend from the time we were six. I was more her sister than Cerise was—*she* was always off in her own little fairyland, all fey and golden and otherworldly. Of course we now know she was apparently boinking half the village."

"Only Richard and Marcel," Manon said.

Axelle waved a hand. "Uh-huh. How many people were you boinking? Or me? None. Because nice girls didn't. Even naughty nice girls didn't. But anyway, I was practically Melita's sister, but she didn't share her power with me. She could have made me stronger, and she didn't. I was the person she loved best in the world, and she left me behind in the dust, just like she left all of you."

"Huh," Manon said thoughtfully.

Axelle wished she'd never started talking; she hated Manon knowing how hurt she felt now, today, at what Melita had done more than two centuries ago. But she couldn't help herself—these last two days had been a revelation.

"I mean, I was proud of her all those years. Yes, maybe I was also envious, but mostly I was proud. And she told me how sorry she was that she couldn't just wave her wand and tell me how to do it, that she had no idea what had happened to her—that maybe she had been born that way. Yeah, right!"

Now that Axelle had gotten started, she couldn't stop. "She *wasn't* born that way—she discovered it. Or someone showed her, someone none of us knew about. If she had shown me, we could have made incredible magick together. But she kept it all to herself."

Manon was watching her now as the implications of this started to sink in.

"And you were best friends," she said.

"More than best friends. Blood sisters." Axelle felt her cheeks heating up with anger, or maybe it was the vodka. For so many years she had let these thoughts go. But now they were stuck in her craw, a constant irritant. "But she didn't want a blood sister—she wanted a *lackey*. She wanted me to stay *beneath* her. She *wanted* to leave me behind. I never would have done that to her." Axelle tipped the glass back angrily. She'd already said too much.

She was pissed, really pissed, at Melita for the first time. She'd hated Melita for leaving her behind, but she hadn't really known what had happened. Maybe something bad had happened to her— maybe she hadn't been able to come back, maybe she hadn't become immortal for some reason, maybe she was dead.

But now Axelle felt, deeply and certainly, that Melita wasn't dead, that she could have taken Axelle with her. She could have shared her power, could have helped Axelle be much stronger—and she had decided to keep Axelle down.

Clio

I woke up feeling like I'd spent the night in a cement mixer.

My alarm sounded like the world coming apart. Groaning, I leaned over and smacked it off the table. Then I looked at the floor, spinning crazily, and realized I was going to hurl.

Our small bathroom was between my room and Thais's, and I stumbled toward it, whacking my shoulder hard on the door frame. I drew in my breath with a hiss, kicked the door shut behind me, and *almost* made it to the john before I tossed. Operative word being *almost*.

After I was done heaving, I splashed water on my face and rinsed out my mouth. A quick look in the mirror told me I looked horrible—splotchy, greenish, hollow-eyed. My birthmark stuck out against my unnaturally pale skin as if someone had smashed a raspberry against my left cheek. I grabbed a towel and swiped up the floor and toilet as best I could, then pushed the towel behind the big, old-fashioned tub, figuring I'd get it later and slip it into the wash.

I felt like walking death. Or in my case, staggering death.

This was a hangover, but the worst effing hangover I'd ever had in my whole misspent youth. This was a hangover caused by doing risky magick. *Dark magick*, I admitted to myself with a searing sense of shame and remorse. Magick I was hiding from Nan and especially Thais.

But that burst of power I'd gotten from the crystal—

My throat tightened again. I grabbed my hair with one hand to keep it out of the line of fire and hunkered over the toilet.

"Clio? Time to get up!" Nan's voice came dimly to me from downstairs.

Oh goddess, I had school today. *Frick.*

"Coming," I croaked, hoping she could hear me.

A couple of dry heaves later, I groped my way to the bathroom door and headed downstairs, hanging onto the handrail so I wouldn't fall and break my neck. Obviously I had "an awful stomach bug," and Nan would definitely let me stay home from school.

The smell of coffee and toast almost made me hurl again, but I forced myself into the kitchen so I could evoke as much sympathy as possible.

"Clio?" Nan called again. "Thais, maybe you should—"

"Hey," I said weakly, entering the kitchen.

"Honey, what's the matter?"

Thais was pouring me a cup of coffee, but she turned around at Nan's tone.

45

"Whoa," she said. "What's wrong?"

"I don't know," I said miserably, and right then I truly did feel miserable, and scared, and deeply ill down to my bones. Tears welled up in my eyes, and I rested my head on the table. If they knew . . .

Nan put a cool hand on my forehead. I had the sudden fear that she would feel the dark vibrations, left in my skin like a scent.

"Hmm—you don't feel feverish," she said, looking at me with concern. "Let me get you something to settle your stomach."

"Yes, please," I said with feeling. "I ate something at Racey's last night—maybe it was bad. Maybe I should call her and see if anyone over there is sick." Still able to think on my feet.

"What did you eat?" Thais asked, coming to sit next to me. "You want some plain toast?"

My stomach recoiled, and I grimaced. "Um, a taco. And no thanks."

Five minutes later I was carefully sipping tea made with fennel, ginger, honey, and ground aniseed, still feeling like death might be a good option at this point. I didn't know why I felt so wretched and wondered if Daedalus did too. Maybe one got used to the effects of dark magick. Right now I never wanted to find out.

"Sip that slowly, honey," said Nan, and sat back down to read the newspaper.

"I don't think I can go to school today," I ventured.

"No, not if you're this sick. Thais can get your

assignments. Another good thing about having a sister."

I looked at Thais, who gave me an overdone perky nod.

"Yep," she said brightly. "I know you don't want to fall behind."

Nan gave me a knowing smile, and I moaned and hung my head over my tea. My stomach felt a tiny bit better.

"Oh, goodness," said Nan, reading the newspaper. "Your school—they've done asbestos testing and have found that some of the old insulation contains asbestos."

"It's an old building," said Thais, finishing her coffee.

Nan kept reading, one hand absently breaking off pieces of cinnamon toast. It smelled really good, and I started to wonder if I could maybe handle a small piece. Then my head throbbed again, a wave of exhaustion came over me, and I decided against it.

"Listen to this," said Nan. "Because they've found evidence of old asbestos, they need to shut the school down for several days while they determine whether they need to rip it all out or if they can just seal it up."

Thais's face lit. "We don't have school?"

This was too good to be true.

"Not for the rest of the week," said Nan, frowning as she read. "They'll make an announcement tonight on the school's web site about what will happen next week. If they actually need to rip out the asbestos, they'll try to divide up the classes and house you all in other buildings, like at Tulane or Loyola."

"Yes," I said gratefully, and drank more tea.

"Wow," said Thais. "Back in Welsford, there were a grade school and a courthouse that had asbestos. They just sealed it all up, though."

"Well, you two have gotten a reprieve," said Nan. She still sounded tired, not totally herself, and I wondered again what had happened to her and Daedalus during the rite.

"Excellent!" said Thais. "No school!"

I remembered to be Clio. "So I'm wasting a perfectly good illness. Way unfair."

Nan sent me a tolerant look, one I knew well. "The injustice. Go on back to bed, honey. I'll come check on you in a little while. Is that tea helping?"

"Yeah. I'll take it up with me. Thanks." I carried it upstairs, feeling like I was made of glass and might splinter apart at any moment. I'd never felt this bad from a regular hangover, not that I'd had many. One night of throwing up cuba libres through my nose had pretty much taught me how to cut off my liquor intake before it got to that point.

This felt much worse, like my *soul* had a hangover. What had I done?

I set the tea on my bedside table and crawled back under the covers. Thank God there was no school—the universe was looking out for me. I wanted to sleep for a year and then wake up to find life back to normal.

I felt Thais coming closer, then heard her foot-steps on the stairs. I closed my eyes when she came in and gently sat down on my bed. If she suspected that I'd started studying with Daedalus, she would be so mad. And worse, so hurt.

"Where were you last night?" she asked.

I opened my eyes. "Racey's. I told you."

She nodded. I couldn't tell if she believed me or not.

"Too bad about Luc's face," she said.

I watched her expression, which looked guarded. As mine probably did.

"Yeah. Bastard."

"Yeah. Anyway, Petra seemed to think it was only temporary. So—" Suddenly her eyes met mine, sharp and green. "Richard. I think he's hot for you."

"What?" I practically yelped, my heart starting to race. "Richard and I can't stand each other."

Except for when we were locked together, our mouths fused, our hands all over each other . . . But Thais didn't know about that. No one did, except me and him.

"I don't know," she persisted. "I saw how he was looking at you. He looked . . . like he wanted to eat you up."

"I don't know what you're talking about," I bluffed. "He's so . . . supercilious. Like he's always sneering."

"Yeah," Thais said thoughtfully. "Well, watch him the next time he's around. See if you notice anything." She stood up. "I can't believe there's no school! I'm going out. Petra still looks kind of under the weather—I'll see if she needs anything. What about you? You want some ginger ale or something?"

"No thanks. I've got this." I gestured to the tea. "What are you going to go do?"

"Go to the grocery store, other stuff," she said vaguely, heading out the door. "Hope you feel better—I'll see you later."

"Okay." Once she left, I snuggled down under my covers again, trying not to cry, knowing I would only feel worse if I did.

So Thais thought Richard was hot for me. I had an image of myself lying on the cool wooden floor of his apartment after I had furiously and unsuccessfully tried to take him apart. After the hitting and screaming and crying I had lain there like a sack of laundry, and he had said, "I don't love you. I don't love anybody. But I see the value of you, the incredible worth of you, more than anyone I've ever known."

Now, lying here in my bed, knowing what I had done last night, how I had taken something beautiful and utterly destroyed it for my own purpose, I started weeping silently. Richard was wrong. I had no value and no worth.

Thais

We didn't have anything like Botanika back in Welsford. I'm sure occult bookstore–coffee shops existed in Connecticut, but I'd never been in one. I wasn't totally comfortable here, still felt like an imposter somehow, among the nose rings and dreadlocks and pink and blue hair. There were some normal-looking people too. But I was pretty much the most boring person here.

Botanika took up the whole front half, almost a block long, of a building that looked like it had been a department store back in the thirties. Huge glass windows overlooked the street, and the interior hinted at what it might have looked like eighty years ago, with pressed-tin ceilings painted a dark copper color, ceiling fans on long poles, all connected to each other by pulleys, and tall columns supporting a roof that must have been eighteen or twenty feet high.

Inside, all the way to the right, was the coffee shop, with its small square black tables and old-fashioned library chairs. Each table had a green-shaded banker's lamp, and the whole place was wi-fi, which explained all the students with laptops.

In the middle section, right when you came in, was a small area with funky clothes, bookshelves lined with all kinds of alternative books, and other shelves with candles, incense, herbs, and oils.

To the far left was a smaller section, less well lit, with more shelves of books. These were more serious, books about witchcraft and voodoo, with detailed information on herbs and stars and the tarot. These were for scholars, people who practiced the craft. The books out front were more for dabblers, people who were curious but not necessarily serious.

At the back of the darker section was an area that was actually restricted. Two rows of bookcases faced each other, with a gold cord across the opening and a sign saying that no one under eighteen was allowed in.

It was easy to duck under.

After the rite, I'd been so upset about Daedalus and what I should do. I couldn't believe Clio didn't feel the same way. But my huge emotions had boiled down into one cold, coherent thought: revenge. I was here to figure out what form that revenge could take. After seeing Luc, I'd thought about doing something like that, only permanent. But Daedalus didn't seem like he would care about his looks much. Daedalus was all about power.

So I wanted to take his away from him.

Of course, I had no idea how to pull it off. As

Clio had pointed out just yesterday, I wasn't a trained witch. I did have some power, and Clio and I together had tons of power, but she'd made it clear I would be doing this alone. This was my first recon trip—I needed to do research, figure out what was involved. If there was anything that I could do now, I would. If it was something that would take years of training, well, I probably had the time.

The books on these shelves looked older, beat up, as if their lives had been hard. Who knew how many generations of witches had used these books and for what purposes? They were loosely organized, but nothing was labeled *Dark Magick (Revenge)*.

I started pulling things out. There were books about garden spells, crop spells, spells that used the moon phases, spells based in herbs or crystals or other tools. A few of the books had spells that seemed kind of dark—like how to make your neighbor's crop fail while yours thrived. But nothing seemed big enough, specific or ruthless enough.

One by one I examined titles, and again and again I had to stop myself from getting lost in something fascinating that didn't relate to my mission. There was a whole book about how women could use spells in conjunction with their monthly cycles, drawing on their changing power. Who knew if that was real or not, but it would be so awesome to read. I had to flip through as many books as possible before someone kicked me out. Next month I would be eighteen, but they probably didn't care about that today.

Finally I saw a book with *Beware* written on its spine in faded, flaking gold leaf. I pulled it out carefully and opened it, half expecting its pages to crumble into dust in front of me. In fact, inside, its ink was so faded that I could barely make out words on the pages. Frustrated, aware of time ticking by, I rifled the pages with my thumb, wishing that suddenly one page would be totally clear and exactly what I needed.

Which didn't happen. All that happened was a small piece of folded paper fluttered out from between the pages and seesawed its way to the dark green linoleum floor. I picked it up and of course opened it. Maybe it was an ancient shopping list. Maybe a love note from someone.

It was an address, scrawled in faded pencil, hard to make out. It said, *Mama Loup's*. I didn't recognize the address. Which meant nothing, because I was still finding my way around this city and constantly got lost on the meandering streets. I slid the book back onto its shelf, ducked under the gold rope again, and headed to the front door, where a stand held tourist stuff in case someone happened to wander in off the sidewalk.

I pulled out a map of New Orleans and looked up the street, just out of curiosity. I mean, I'd found it in a book called *Beware*, in the restricted section of Botanika. The street turned out to be really short, maybe three blocks long, stuck between two longer streets that framed it like the letter *H*. It was on the edge of the Quarter, close to Rampart and Esplanade.

I decided to go.

It took me a while to find it, despite having looked at a map. I drove down the block, looking for a parking space, and I noticed how run-down everything looked here. New Orleans in general seemed to have a laissez-faire attitude toward litter and keeping public spaces tidy, but I was always shocked when I went through the poorer neighborhoods and saw how incredibly third world they looked. I was equally shocked by the fact that no one seemed to think this was unusual or alarming.

This was one of those streets. Only four blocks from the bustling French Quarter, with its tour buses disgorging tourists by the thousands, this street seemed far removed from anyone's attention. It was distinctly run-down, with crumpled wire hurricane fences sagging on their posts, trash and weedy brown grass clumps everywhere. It was mostly residential, and the houses here were small and unkept, with tiny, raggedy yards, peeling paint, shutters lurching on one hinge.

After circling the block, I took a parking spot on the street that had at first seemed too far but now appeared to be a reasonable option. I sat in the car for a moment and said every protection spell I could remember of the ones Petra had taught me. I tried to protect the pathetic tin-can rental car, myself, the air around me, and so on. I was aware of people walking by, looking at me, a white anomaly in their neighborhood of color.

I read the numbers on the address again, then

got out of my car, locked it, and headed down the street. The address led me to a regular house, and I stood in front of it, frowning. Then I noticed it wasn't a totally regular house. A strip of broken sidewalk led around the side, and there was a crude, handwritten sign that said *Mama Loup's* with an arrow pointing toward the back. As I was wondering what to do, a woman came down the side alley and walked past me.

"You can go on if you want," she said in a friendly voice, gesturing toward the back, then passed me through the rusted iron gate.

"Okay," I said, still hesitating. Then I thought, *If I can't even walk down a slightly spooky alley in broad daylight, how can I ever expect to take revenge on one of the world's most powerful witches?* Did I want to do this or not? Had I thought it was going to be easy? That it would be clean and fun and light?

Feeling disgusted with my lameness, I strode down the alley. Ragged bamboo fencing made a six-foot screen to one side, hiding the house from its neighbor. At that moment, the sun blinked out. I stopped and looked up to see that rolling thunderclouds had filled the sky. Great. Because this place didn't have enough atmosphere.

A man came out, letting a screen door slam behind him. He brushed past me fast in the alley, head down.

I stopped in front of the door. A single lightbulb in a rusted fixture hung crookedly over the doorway. The door needed painting, and the screen had several holes rusted out. I couldn't see anything behind the screen. I swallowed hard and pulled it open.

I stepped in, unable to focus on anything. Blinking rapidly, I stayed right inside the screen, ready to leap backward if I heard something—the sound of a gun cocking, for example. Oh God, I was so scared. I suddenly thought of everything bad that could happen to me here, of how stupid I'd been, of how I was going to end up floating down the river, Jane Doe—

"You need help, sugar?" someone asked, and I almost screamed and leaped into the air. The southern accent was so strong I could hardly understand it.

"Uh," I said, looking around wildly. Now I could see things, I realized. Shelves and posters on the walls and another bare lightbulb casting a weak light over in the corner.

"You looking for something? You lost?" The voice seemed bemused by my presence, but not unkind.

"I was looking for Mama Loup's," I said, my voice wavering.

"You done found it, honey. Whatcha want with Mama Loup?"

The shelves held candles of all colors. Some of them were shaped like people. Or body parts. Including a—

"Need a spell," I mumbled, my eyes taking in the old posters thumbtacked to the bead-board walls. I saw a faded, ripped one for a concert, a band called the Radiators.

"What kind of spell?"

Now I focused on the person talking to me. It was a woman somewhere between the ages of thirty and sixty. A brightly colored kerchief covered her hair. She wore African-style robes of intricately patterned material and plastic flip-flops on her feet. One hand held a feather duster, which she had been flicking over the shelves.

"Honey, you want like a love spell for your boyfriend?" She was amused now, starting to head toward a cracked glass counter case. "He foolin' around on you? You want him back? Want to make him sorry? I got what you need."

"No," I said, barely audibly. I cleared my throat. *Get it done, Thais.* "No," I said more clearly. "I need a spell to strip a witch's power from him."

The woman paused halfway behind the counter and looked at me. Adrenaline had flooded my veins, and my heart felt like it would pump right out of my chest. I stepped closer, trying to look strong and unafraid.

"I'm a witch," I said firmly, hoping it wasn't a lie. "Another witch has wronged me. I want to strip his power away, leave him like an empty shell."

The woman blinked, then looked me up and down, as if a stuffed animal had suddenly started talking to her.

I don't know what made me do this, but I stepped closer still and touched my fingers to the back of her hand. I had to convince her, make her help me. I looked deeply into her eyes, concentrating on the power flowing from my fingertips.

Her brown eyes widened. She stared down at my hand, then looked up at my face. I saw her gaze rest on my birthmark for several seconds. She was solemn now, not joking, not patronizing.

I saw her thinking, felt her indecision. I waited, trying to calm my breathing.

She drew her hand away, looking uncertain, then murmured, "Wait a minute." Turning, she went through a hanging bamboo curtain that almost concealed a doorway behind the counter.

I waited. No one else came into the shop. The air was full of incense that tickled my nose and throat. My eyes had adjusted, but everything still seemed unusually dim, as if light was actually being sucked out of the room. I'd gone from terror to a milder, barely controlled panic.

"Hello."

The voice came from behind me—I hadn't heard or sensed anyone nearby. Whirling, I came face-to-face with another dark woman. I couldn't make out her features—it was as if she wore a thin, invisible veil over her face.

"Mama Loup says you need a spell."

My voice was gone. So this was not Mama Loup, then.

"My name is Carmela," she went on. I couldn't make out her accent or whether she was black or white or Hispanic.

"I'm—" I began automatically, then stopped. Give a fake name?

"What are you looking for?"

"Someone killed my father," I got out, the words sounding harsh and bald in that quiet room. "I want revenge. He's a witch. I want to strip his powers from him."

Suddenly this all seemed so impossible, so unbelievable. What was I doing? Who was I? This wasn't even *me*.

"You believe in witches, then?"

"I have to. I am one." Oh God, what if this was a cop or something? Was I doing something illegal? Was this a trap? *Get me out of here!*

"And this witch wronged you?"

"He killed my father. I want to destroy him."

"Destroy but not kill?"

Going into the Treize's immortality would be too much. "Losing his powers would be worse than dying to him."

"Yes," the woman murmured, moving away from me. "It would be, for a witch."

She walked slowly through the shop, as though thinking things over. Every once in a while I felt her dark eyes on me. I prayed a SWAT team wasn't about to bust in here. All I wanted was to run screaming down that alleyway, out to the open street and my car. *Let me make it out of here alive*, I prayed, holding my breath.

"A spell that would strip his powers away is dark magick."

No duh, I thought with rising hysteria.

"It's very dark magick. You'll bear a mark on your soul forever."

"He killed my father." I felt like tears were not far away.

"I will teach you a spell," the woman said, "if you are truly determined to do this. It won't be easy. Are you prepared for pain? For fear? For darkness?"

His or mine? "Yes," I said, quaking.

"You will need these supplies. Come back when you have them."

A slip of thick gray paper seemed to materialize out of the air.

I took it, my hand shaking. "Okay," I barely whispered.

"Go home, little girl," she said. "Do not come back until you're ready."

"Okay." I nodded. Then, without waiting for her to say anything else, I wove my way through the dimness to the screen door and its patch of gray light leading to the outside. I crashed my way out, flinging aside the door and then breaking into a run down the alleyway. The air felt heavy and still, but so much fresher and more real than the air inside Mama Loup's.

What had I done?

Damned All Over Again

Marcel wished services were still in Latin. How much more majestic they had been, more mysterious, seeming truly more divine than human. Now everything was in everyday English, boring, pedestrian. Impossible to communicate the glory and terrifying omnipotence of the Christian God.

Marcel winced. He meant God. His God. The One God.

Deep in his soul, he still had doubts.

This church was pretty, St. Louis Cathedral, right on Jackson Square. He remembered when this one, the third church to stand on this spot, had been built in 1849. It still held daily masses and three services on Sundays.

The sparse congregation, consisting of a handful of ancient women in black veils, some tourists, and a couple of nuns in modern habits, stood. Marcel stood with them. People opened hymnals, but Marcel had no need to. He had memorized everything in the hymnal and the Book of Common Prayer decades ago. Sometimes the wording was updated, modernized, but Marcel always found his footing again.

The priest and altar servers made their way down the wide middle aisle, singing the final closing. Marcel filed out behind them, heading out into an afternoon that had clouded over and dropped about eight degrees. Which meant it was about seventy-eight. Welcome to October.

Marcel kept walking, through Jackson Square and across the street to Café du Monde. Having done today's penance, he could indulge in coffee and beignets, a silly, childish treat. And completely inconsequential, compared to a lifetime of burning in a Christian hell.

He was standing inside the outdoor railing, looking for a vacant table, when he heard his name called.

"Marcel!" When he looked over, his stomach knotted. Claire and Jules. He'd always liked Jules, liked his quiet dignity.

But what Jules saw in Claire, Marcel would never know.

There was no avoiding them; they'd seen him and were waving him over.

"Hello," he said stiffly, pulling out a chair and sitting down. A tiny Vietnamese waitress hurried over and he gave her his order.

Claire took a bite of beignet, sending powdered sugar raining down. The server brought Marcel's coffee and his own three beignets, and he took a deep breath, inhaling the rich coffee scent, tempered with chicory and made with boiled milk. The best coffee anywhere.

"So, Marcel," Claire said, still chewing. "Looks like heaven spit you back out again, eh?"

Jules paused in mid-bite, his dark eyes turning to look at her.

Marcel also froze. Trust Claire to be the bull in a china shop. He didn't answer her but blew on his coffee and took a sip.

"I'm just saying," said Claire. "I mean, what were you thinking? Jesus, if a measly knife in the heart would do it, you think I wouldn't have checked out long ago?"

"Claire." Jules frowned.

She looked at him impatiently. "Come on, you know it's true. And I'm not the only one." She turned back to Marcel. "What made you think it would possibly work?"

Again a black, bleak depression settled on Marcel. His chest actually still hurt where the knife had gone in. He'd been so hopeful, so ready to die. And then to find out he was cursed to continue walking the earth for who knew how long . . .

"I thought the power from the rite," he got out with difficulty, then prevented himself from saying more by biting into his hot doughnut. It was, as usual, as close to heaven as he would probably ever get.

"Well, it's not gonna be that easy," Claire said. "That bastard pulled us all here for his big magic show—like we're effing puppets—and then he's all surprised when lo and behold, not everyone's being their most cooperative. Idiot."

Marcel glanced at Jules over the rim of his heavy china coffee cup. Jules was pretty much Daedalus's oldest confidant. It was a somewhat unlikely alliance, but Marcel knew they'd been traveling together, studying together, off and on for about a hundred years.

"Daedalus is very ambitious," Jules said now. "He feels that he—that all of us—were wronged during Melita's rite, and he wants to repair what he can, enhance what he can—in essence restore some kind of balance to our lives."

Claire looked at Jules for a minute. She leaned over and put her hand gently against his cheek. "Dear, sweet, naive Jules," she said in a honeyed voice. "Yes, I'm *sure* that's it. I'm sure Daedalus is trying to *restore balance to our lives*." She dropped her hand and rolled her eyes while Jules looked uncomfortable. "You guys—Daedalus has *never*, in his long, controlling, avaricious life, *ever* done *anything* for someone else—unless it benefited him somehow."

Marcel watched Jules, watched the emotions cross his face. Jules looked like he wanted to refute Claire's words but seemed to realize that example after example proved her right.

Claire ate another doughnut, as though she had all the time in the world for Jules's illusions to be stripped away one by one.

"Then what do you think he's doing?" Marcel asked.

"He wants to re-create the rite. Why, I don't know. I think we need to find out." She looked at Jules meaningfully, but he stared straight ahead and drank his coffee. "Maybe he just wants more power. Maybe he's trying to pull Melita back. Maybe it'll reverse our immortality but extend his. I don't know. I just know I'm getting more pissed by the day, being here. I tried to go over to the coast yesterday to visit some friends, and I got as far as Ocean Springs before his spell kicked in and I had to turn around." She sounded very bitter.

"I just want this to end," Marcel said quietly.

"Your life should be celebrated." Jules looked serious, despite the tiny bit of powdered sugar dotting his lip. "All life should be celebrated. You've been given a gift—the chance to rejoice every day, to do whatever you want to give your life meaning."

"Here it comes," Claire muttered.

"Both of you—so caught up in yourselves," Jules went on. "Instead of sitting around being unhappy, why don't you do something to give your life purpose?"

"Orphans in Africa," Claire said under breath.

"There are people all over the world who need help," Jules said earnestly.

"I know," Marcel said, feeling defensive. "I've been taking care of the poor in Ireland for the last hundred and forty years."

"And that didn't give your life meaning?" Jules asked. "Didn't it give you some measure of joy, to know you were making a difference in those desolate lives?"

"It was all right."

Jules let out a deep breath. "You have been granted the opportunity to live extraordinary lives. Quit wasting them." He stood abruptly and dropped some money on the table for a tip. With a last, unreadable look at Claire, he made his way through the crowded tables and disappeared toward the levee.

"That's Jules for you," Claire said, sounding not at all bothered by his lecture. "Sincere as shit. Still—" Her eyes followed his broad back. "He's a good person." Her voice sounded uncharacteristically soft, affectionate, and Marcel looked at her curiously.

"What is it with you and Jules?" he surprised himself by asking.

Claire looked surprised too, that Marcel would address it so openly.

"Oh, you know." She waved her hand vaguely, watching the crowd where Jules could no longer be seen. "I love him. He won't have me. And so on.

"But the question is," she said, looking at Marcel shrewdly, "what are we going to do about Daedalus?"

"What *can* we do?"

"You know who we should talk to?" Claire asked. "Axelle. Our Axelle has become quite the power-house."

Thais

"You're gonna love this place," Kevin said, patting my knee before shifting gears.

"Good—I'm hungry." I looked over at him and smiled, trying to seem normal. This had been such a bizarre week. Kevin had been wanting to get together every day. I'd missed him, but he seemed so removed from the rest of my life—there was so much I couldn't share with him. Or with Clio, or Petra. Meeting Carmela, starting on that path, was weighing heavily on me, like a heavy, dark cloak that I couldn't take off. What would Clio and Petra say if they knew?

I looked out the Miata's window, seeing the shadows slanting steeply from the tall oak trees. It was as hot as summer, but the sunlight looked autumny: its quality, its angle. Every day I stepped outside, expecting a crispness in the air—and every day I was disappointed. Back home I'd be wearing sweaters by now and a jacket at night.

"And no school next week!" Kevin smacked his hands against the steering wheel. "How cool is that? Let's get Sylvie and Claude and go do something tomorrow, maybe get a little sailboat, have a picnic out on the lake."

"That sounds great," I said, loving the idea of doing something so ordinary. With Kevin, I got a glimpse of my old life, when I'd been a regular teenager in a regular town. More and more I felt like I was leaving him behind—and last night, at Mama Loup's . . .

"You cold?" Kevin's face was concerned, and he adjusted the AC. "You're shivering."

"No, I'm fine," I said. "Thanks."

"Hey—are you all right?" He steered with one hand, lacing the other through mine on my lap. Every so often he released it to shift; then he'd take it back. "You seem kind of . . . distracted."

"I'm sorry," I said. "It's been a crazy week. I haven't been getting much sleep, and my grandmother seems to be getting sick or something. I'm having a hard time focusing."

"That's okay—I know how those crazy weeks go."

I bet you don't, I thought.

"Is there anything I can do to help?"

He was literally the sweetest guy I'd ever met. I gave him a bigger smile.

"No, this is good, right here. Getting po'boys with you and then a movie. It's just what I need. A perfect Friday night." Nope, no witches here.

"Okay. But anything you want, you tell me."

"Thanks—you're a sweetie."

Kevin smiled at my endearment, then turned off Magazine Street toward the river. The houses here were small but mostly nicely kept. Kids were playing, and dogs were running around barking.

I got lost in my thoughts for a moment, these small houses such a contrast to the ones I had seen just yesterday. Yesterday. That whole experience had shaken me to the core. I'd made the decision to start down a dark path, a decision that would mark my soul forever, according to Carmela. And when witches said "dark," they meant really *dark*, good-versus-evil kind of stuff. Stuff that could, well, mark your soul forever.

Was I ready to do it? This morning I'd bought some of the supplies from Carmela's list at Botanika. The clerk had looked at the assembled pile and then examined my face, as if to judge whether I should be buying this stuff. Some things I'd been able to get from Nan's cabinet in the workroom, very quietly, when I was supposed to be in there studying.

I'd felt weird and kind of off all day. Now I seized a chance to feel normal and innocent.

"Where are we going?" I asked, seeing nothing but houses, no businesses anywhere.

"Around the corner," Kevin said. "It's a little hole in the wall, but they make the best roast beef po'boys anywhere."

"Sounds great," I began, but at that moment, a little girl chased a puppy into the street, right in front of us. I gasped, and time seemed to slow down, each second taking thirty seconds to get through.

"Whoa!" Kevin said, and jerked the steering

wheel to one side, but not far enough. The little girl, maybe four years old, froze with fear, staring at us. Someone yelled from the sidewalk, and I think someone leaped up toward the street. Words came into my mind, and I repeated them unquestioningly. Not knowing why, I put my hands together like an arrow, then split them apart fast, as if sending a burst of air between our car and the little girl.

The next moment, she was blown backward, right out of the street and against the curb, where she landed with a small skid. The puppy was flung to the opposite side with a startled, high-pitched yelp. An adult dropped next to the child, gathering her up into strong arms. She started wailing.

"Oh my God," I exclaimed, watching all this happen. "That was close!" Then I realized that our car was still moving, listing to one side of the street. "Kevin?"

Next to me, Kevin's head hung limply toward one shoulder. His hands had fallen off the steering wheel, and his eyes were closed. The car jumped the curb with a jolt, and I grabbed the wheel just in time for us to hit a fire hydrant on the corner.

Wham! I was jerked forward. My seat belt caught hard and slammed me back into my seat. I felt shaken like a rag doll. When I looked at Kevin, he looked dead.

"Kevin! Kevin!" I grabbed one shoulder and shook it, and he blinked groggily.

Then, just like in the movies, I heard a loud rushing sound, and a geyser of water shot out of

71

the broken fire hydrant, shooting twenty feet in the air, then dropping heavily onto the hood and roof of our car.

"Wha?" Kevin mumbled. He blinked again, looking around in a daze, and slowly took in my anxious face, the car lurched up onto the sidewalk at an angle, the crashing water.

"What happened?" His voice sounded thick, and his face looked gray.

"What's wrong?" Starting to freak out, I saw that his lips looked faintly blue. I grabbed one of his hands. It was ice cold.

People had gathered around our car, and now the doors opened on both sides.

"Miss, you okay?" A gentle brown hand extended to help me out. On Kevin's side, people were helping him out too, but he sagged against a man, who quickly set him down on the grass by the curb.

"Kevin! My boyfriend!" I said, hurrying over to him, then remembered I had a cell phone. I dialed 911 as fast as I could and started babbling at the calm person on the other end.

"Sit down, honey," said a woman, tugging on my arm, and I sank down moments before my knees gave way.

Someone took the phone out of my hand. While I stroked Kevin's clammy forehead and patted his hand, I heard a heavy southern accent say, "I don't know what happened. This girl and her boyfriend just knocked over a hydrant. Uh-huh." I heard him give an address.

"Get an ambulance!" I said urgently, because Kevin wasn't snapping out of it.

"This girl wants an ambulance," the man repeated. "And her boyfriend don't look so hot, I gotta tell ya."

After that, different choppy scenes intruded into my consciousness. The little girl we'd almost hit was okay, though scraped on one elbow. The puppy was okay. Most of the front end of Kevin's car was crumpled. I got my purse out of the car, then sat down next to Kevin again, holding his hand. I put my other hand on his heart and felt it racing uncontrollably.

Jeez, slow down, I thought fearfully. *Slow down*; calme-toi. Within seconds his heart did seem to slow down, but I didn't know if I had done it.

"What happened to you?" I asked him.

"Don't know." He shook his head, still looking sick and gray.

An ambulance came. Police came. The fire department came and pushed Kevin's car out of the way and sealed the broken hydrant. The police questioned everybody, and I was pretty incoherent. They gave both me and Kevin alcohol tests, which were negative, of course.

One paramedic said, "It's like he got hit by lightning or something. He's seriously out of whack."

The sky was cloudy but there was no thunder, no lightning. They picked Kevin up and strapped him onto a gurney.

I remembered to call Kevin's house and explained

it all to his stepmother, who promised to meet him immediately at the hospital. She urged me to go home and lie down if I felt I didn't need to be seen by a doctor.

"We barely hit the hydrant," I said. "But Kevin was out before we hit it."

Finally they took Kevin to the hospital. I held his hand and kissed his cheek, but he seemed oblivious. A policewoman helped me into a cruiser and drove me home.

And that's when I had the thought—what if this had happened to us, to me, because of what I had set in motion last night?

Thais

"Thank you." I was so glad to be home.

"Let me walk you to your door," said the police-woman as I climbed out of the cruiser.

"No, that's okay, thanks." I was embarrassed that she was seeing me all upset and weak-kneed and just wanted her to go.

As soon as I opened the front door, Petra called, "Thais?"

"Yes." I headed toward the kitchen, practicing sending out my Spidey senses to see if Clio was home. I didn't feel her, but maybe she was upstairs and I couldn't get that far yet.

I stopped in the workroom and concentrated, but my nerves were so jangled, and all I wanted to do was sit down.

In the kitchen, Petra looked the same as when I'd left less than two hours ago: a bit pale, tired. She glanced out the window, seeing what time it was.

"That was quick," she said. "I thought you were going to a movie."

"I was." I headed to the fridge and poured myself a glass of the ever-present iced tea.

"What's wrong, honey? You feel upset."

Startled, I thought, *Like, you're informing me?* Then I realized I felt upset *to her*: my aura felt upset; she could pick up on it. I sighed.

"Well," I began reluctantly, sinking into a kitchen chair. "Something happened to Kevin, and he wrecked his car. And we almost hit a little kid." I collapsed onto the table, my head on my arms.

"What? Goddess, Thais, what happened? Are you okay? Where's Kevin?" Petra immediately got up and came to me, stroking my hair, her long, sensitive fingers tracing my forehead as though to get the information out of me by osmosis.

"I'm okay. Kevin's at the hospital. His stepmom said I should come home."

"But what happened?"

I tried to put it all together in my mind. "We were just driving, not too fast, down a little street. And suddenly a little girl ran in front of our car."

I sat up, trying to remember what had happened in what order. "There was a puppy. She ran after the puppy. She saw us but was too scared to move. I gasped, and Kevin said something and jerked the steering wheel, but there was no way we wouldn't hit her."

"Oh my God," Petra said, rubbing my shoulders.

"Then—I don't know what happened, but I remember thinking I had to stop it somehow. Word just popped into my head, and I said them.

76

And I did this with my hands." I showed Petra the splitting-arrow thing. "And then, boom, the little girl flew over by the sidewalk, and the puppy went in the opposite direction. So we didn't hit them."

I looked up to see a bizarre expression on Petra's face. She focused on me solemnly, as if I'd just given her some terrible news.

"What?" I asked.

"Have you been studying displacement spells?"

"No. What's a—oh, when you move something out of the way? No, you know I haven't. I'm still learning the bazillion words for herbs." I tried not to sound bitter, but the amount of sheer memorization required for the craft was overwhelming.

"You haven't studied anything like that? Has Clio shown you something similar? Or anyone else?"

I thought. "No. I don't know how I knew it. It was just there. What?" I was starting to feel alarmed at Petra's expression.

"Okay," she said, sitting down across from me. "Then what happened?"

"Well, I did the thing, and the little girl was out of the way. But we headed toward the left curb, and I saw that Kevin was unconscious, passed out."

"Unconscious?" Petra looked awful.

"Yeah—I don't know what happened. It's like he's—diabetic or something and just passes out. The paramedics said it was like he'd been hit by lightning. This happened once before," I said, the word *lightning* triggering a memory. "That night we *did* get hit by lightning. Remember? Kevin almost

77

passed out, and that guy had to help us. I mean, I wonder what's wrong with him. Maybe I should talk to his dad or stepmom about it."

Petra gazed at me with her clear, blue-gray eyes. "He's not diabetic," she said.

"How do you know?" Could she really tell without even examining him?

"It's you. It's what happens when you make magick around him."

I stared at her. "What do you mean?"

"I don't know why you're able to perform such powerful spells without studying," Petra said slowly. "But with Kevin—what you're doing is, essentially, sucking his energy out of him. His life force."

Horrified, I gaped at her. "What?"

"Magick doesn't come out of thin air," Petra explained. "Though it might look like it does. Magick is everywhere, and when you make magick, it's mostly *gathering* magick. Though you can increase what you have to work with."

I wasn't following her.

"Trained witches create boundaries around their spells so they don't affect any living thing around them, except of course whatever they want to affect. But you're not trained, and when you do powerful magick, it grabs force from wherever it can. In this case, from Kevin."

I could hardly take it in. "I did that to him? But he was—he was gray. His heart was beating way too fast. He's at the *hospital*."

Petra nodded. "It happened before, at the fountain.

At the time, I thought maybe the lightning itself had affected him. But now it seems like it was probably you."

"Oh my God." I was appalled and felt my throat close and tears spring to my eyes. *I had done that to Kevin.* My making magick had sent him to the hospital. And now all sorts of memories came to me—of Kevin suddenly seeming dizzy a couple of times. Even his stepmother swaying against a door frame. Every time I had called up the tiniest little spell, it had affected him badly. Today the spell had been pretty strong, and it had practically killed him.

"Oh my God," I repeated. "What am I going to do?"

"You have to learn how to put up boundaries as fast as you can," said Petra. "But that can take a long time. Or you have to stop making magick of any kind, for any reason, around Kevin—or any other non-witch, for that matter. Witches have a built-in defense mechanism—you'd have to try really hard to take our power."

I swallowed, not looking at her, steering my mind away from what I wanted to do to Daedalus.

"The third option is, you have to stop seeing Kevin."

Today, last night, this whole week had been too much. I couldn't stand it. "I'm going to take a shower," I said, my voice breaking. Standing up, I didn't even make it through the doorway before I started crying.

"Thais," Petra called.

I turned back and saw her looking very serious.

"You need to make some hard choices," she said, her voice gentle. "But you must make them. Let me know if you need help."

I nodded and headed upstairs. In the bathroom I pulled the shower curtain around the big old-fashioned tub and turned on the water. I lay in the tub, eyes closed, with the water raining down on me as if it could wash away all my darkness.

Another Hundred Years

"I'm not sure she wants to talk to you." Axelle sounded apologetic, but Sophie knew better.

She had come prepared. "I need to speak to Manon now, Axelle."

When Axelle continued to block her apartment door, Sophie brushed past her and entered the cool, dark interior. It was amazing, Sophie thought, how they each managed to find their own environments in whatever city they happened to be living in. Axelle's apartments always looked like this. Daedalus's were unmistakably his. Wherever she and Manon settled, it had always seemed homey and warm, welcoming and safe.

Except now. Now Manon was gone, most of her clothes out of their closet. It felt unbearably bleak and empty, awful to come home to. And she'd been gone only four days.

Axelle's small, dark foyer opened up into the large main room on the right and a small galley kitchen on the left, separated from the hallway by a half counter. A black cat sat on the counter, drinking water from a bowl.

It took a moment for Sophie's eyes to adjust—the kitchen light was on, but the main room was lit by only two inadequate lamps. The first thing she saw was Marcel's bright, copper-penny hair, starkly visible against the black and white of the kitchen. What was he doing here?

"Sophie," he said, nodding at her.

"Hi," she said, flustered, and then turned toward the main room. To her relief she saw Manon, draped over both arms of a big leather chair, reading a *Marie Claire* magazine.

"Hi," Sophie said, hurrying over to her. She sank down beside Manon's chair, gazing up at the face she'd loved for more than a hundred years. Manon looked tired, unhappy, and Sophie wanted to pull her into her arms, hold her tightly, tell her everything was going to be all right. Reaching out, she touched Manon's denim-covered knee, but Manon pulled away. Sophie's heart sank lower.

"Can we talk, please?" she asked in a low voice, all too aware of Marcel and Axelle.

Manon's expression was unforgiving. "We've talked."

Sophie glanced behind her to see Axelle making no effort to disguise the fact that she was listening in. She was making a gin and tonic at the kitchen counter while Marcel watched her, frowning slightly. Why was he here, anyway? He couldn't stand Axelle.

"Please, honey," Sophie said. "Please, let's just talk it out. You know I wouldn't hurt you for the world."

"No, but you would hurt me for *you*," Manon replied quietly.

The words stung. Sophie wanted to deny them, but deep down she knew they were true. She'd been willing to sentence Manon to an endless lifetime of unhappiness and frustration just so that she, Sophie, wouldn't lose her. The really bitter thing was that she hadn't had to do anything at all—they'd seen that even a much more powerful suicide spell wouldn't work. If she had done nothing, if she had even pretended to support Manon's wishes, she would still have had the outcome she wanted.

And Manon wouldn't have left her.

"I'm so sorry," she said, looking down at her hands, clenched in her lap. "I know it was wrong. You're right—it was inexcusably selfish of me. But I did it out of love—because I love you so much I can't bear the thought of living without you."

"That's the thing," Manon said slowly, standing up. Sophie scrambled to her feet, watching the sweet, perfect face that had frozen in time when Manon was thirteen years old. "I believe that you did it because you couldn't bear the thought of living alone. But I don't know if that was about me, really *me*, or just about you being afraid to live alone."

"What are you talking about?" Sophie cried, following Manon to the kitchen. Glancing uncomfortably at Axelle and Marcel, she saw they were watching with undisguised interest. "Manon—can we talk about it in private? Please?"

"I don't want to talk about it at all." Manon's voice was bleak. She got a glass out of a cupboard and helped herself to some gin and tonic. There was a lime already sliced, and Manon squeezed a piece into her drink, then dropped it in.

"You have to forgive me." Sophie was growing ever more alarmed. She and Manon had had fights before—had even broken up for a few days at a time—but that had felt different than this. Manon seemed so cold, so unyielding.

Manon sipped her drink, watching Sophie over the rim. "No, I don't." The words sounded sad rather than angry.

Sophie's heart froze. "Manon—can't you see that I need you? That I love you more than anything?"

"I believe that you need me."

"You think I don't *love* you?" This was beyond humiliation, having to beg like this. But Sophie was past caring. All that mattered was that Manon relented and came back.

"I don't know," said Manon quietly, touching an ice cube with one fingertip, not looking at Sophie. "Maybe you just can't be alone."

"*What?* Manon, how can you say that?" Sophie exclaimed, feeling close to tears. "I love you! You're the only person I've ever loved!" As soon as the words were out of her mouth, she had a cold, sinking feeling. But maybe Manon wouldn't remember . . .

"That's not entirely true," Manon said evenly. "I've had a lot of time to think." She gave a short, bitter laugh. "I mean, a *lot* of time. And now I wonder if I wasn't always second best."

Sophie gaped at her, horrified. *Oh no, oh no, oh no—don't say it, don't go there—*

84

"Compared to how much you loved Marcel."

There was dead silence in the small kitchen. Outside, someone shrieked with laughter; a car horn blared. Sophie felt far removed from this bright, untidy kitchen, with plates piled in the sink, Minou leaning down from a counter, pawing through the trash. She stared at Manon's small, heart-shaped face, aware only of a desperate, desperate hope that she had misheard, that Manon hadn't just said that in front of these two, that Manon would never betray her . . .

. . . the way she had betrayed Manon the night of the rite.

Oh goddess.

Sophie pressed her hand to her mouth, feeling like she was going to be sick.

"Whaaat?" Axelle asked with fascination, her black eyes darting from Manon to Marcel to Sophie.

Sophie couldn't move, couldn't believe this was happening. She took rapid, shallow breaths, aware of Axelle and Marcel on either side of her in her periphery. Her eyes were locked on Manon's sad, angry, ashamed, triumphant face.

"Uh . . ." said Marcel, sounding shocked.

What was he doing? Thinking back over the last 240 years, looking for clues? Sophie thought hysterically.

"My God," said Axelle softly. "None of us knew. Except Manon."

"I have to go," Sophie breathed through clenched jaws. Blindly she turned and stumbled toward the front door. Her car keys jingled in one pocket; she had no idea where her purse was. It didn't matter. Nothing mattered anymore. She clawed frantically at the locks, yanked the door open, and ran out into the courtyard. A motion sensor light came on, flashing white light into her face. Sophie shaded her eyes and ran down the flagstone alley to the street. She tried to remember where she had parked, but her mind was a complete blank. Instead she hurried down one block and then another, not knowing where she was going, not caring.

She couldn't believe Manon had done that to her. Now Marcel knew. Manon might be giving them all the details even now, details Sophie had confided to her more than a hundred years ago, in the early stages of their affair.

Finally she collapsed against an old brick wall overhung with long canes of a Lady Banks rose, trailing to the sidewalk. Pressing her face against the soft orange brick, Sophie sobbed.

This, more than anything, meant that she and Manon were over for good.

This time last year, I'd been juggling three different guys, including a twenty-two-year-old paralegal I'd met at Amadeo's. Every Friday and Saturday night had been taken; I'd been so busy I could hardly catch my breath.

Look at me this year: my only romance in the last three months had ended in humiliating disaster. Other than that, I had the occasional, incendiary smash-mouth with Richard, who I didn't like and who didn't like me.

Now here I was on a Saturday morning, in a cemetery, with a man old enough to be my grandfather, like, a million times over. Yet this seemed more important than social butterflying—not that anyone would ever believe I thought that.

"Okay, now, is the whole earth going to crumble into lifeless powder when I do this?" I sounded grumpy, probably to hide my fear and distaste. The last time I'd done this, a beautiful crystal had turned to horrible, dead-feeling powder in my hand because I'd taken its life force. Its energy. Its chi. You might think a crystal is already pretty dead, and yeah, it isn't alive in the same way that a squirrel is, or a freshman, or an amoeba. But magickally, there's a huge, striking, palpable difference between a regular crystal, solid and integral, and what had been left after I'd taken its chi. The powder had felt repulsive to me, dead. I'd thought about it since then and decided it felt like anti-life, anti-magick. Not just *nothing*, but a horrible absence of something. It had been like holding death, and it made my skin crawl.

Which made my sitting here, getting ready to do it on a bigger scale, seem astoundingly stupid, even for me.

"No," said Daedalus. "We can set the limitations to exclude actual vertebrates and invertebrates so the energy will come solely from plants and the earth itself. Nothing will turn to white powder, I assure you."

I nodded, thinking about Thais and Nan. They would hate my being here. Since I'd started studying with Daedalus, I'd been hiding it every moment I was home. Usually when I felt bad, I'd go to Nan for help. I could even go to Thais, my sister. But not about this. Not about how sick this made me or how it felt emotionally. This I just had to handle on my own. It separated me from them like nothing else.

"The last time I did this," I told Daedalus as he continued to set up the spell, "I had the mother of all hangovers. I barfed my guts up, which doesn't do much for a girl's looks. What caused that?"

"Everything has a price, Clio," Daedalus said,

trickling salt in a circle around us. This was a little-visited corner of the cemetery, with fine, short grass and the occasional weed popping up next to the crypts. Daedalus had set up a couple of spells to gently turn people aside if they came close to us and to make us hard to see if they somehow got through anyway.

"It will grow less with time," he went on. "I can also give you some herbs and a spell to help counter the aftereffects. But if you want to sail through with your beauty rituals and your make-him-love-me tisanes, then you've come to the wrong place."

His voice was suddenly harsh, his face forbidding. Now I felt like a wuss for even mentioning it.

"Whatever," I snapped. We worked in silence for ten minutes, Daedalus doing his parts and me doing mine. When everything was set up, we sat cross-legged in the circle, facing each other. A heavy black pillar candle rested in its holder between us.

"You'll be drawing energy up out of the earth," Daedalus explained. "The earth is humming with the vibrations of the living things within it, of the life and growth and change happening on a huge scale and a minuscule scale, at every second. Deep, deep beneath the surface, where not even bacteria can live, you still have the energy of the earth itself, its inner core of burning iron."

I looked at him. "You couldn't tap into that. It'd be like tapping into a nuclear bomb."

"Yes," said Daedalus, sounding regretful. "It would take the strongest magick imaginable and would probably end up killing you. I'm just pointing it out. Now, are you ready? Do you remember the first part of the spell?"

Nodding, I let my hands rest palms up on my knees. This position is used a lot in meditation because it connects all the parts of your body to all the other parts, creating a circle of energy. Meditation and magick have a lot to do with each other.

It was much like it was before. The first part of the spell set the limitations and defined the scope of the spell. The second part put me in touch with my own personal power. The third part sought out and identified other magickal power, in this case, from within the earth, the actual dirt, beneath us. And the *fin-quatrième* aligned the two powers, joining my energy with the earth's.

At first nothing seemed to happen, and I was disappointed. Then, just like when the charcoal briquettes caught on fire, I became aware of power licking at the edges of my consciousness.

"Open yourself to it," Daedalus murmured, his eyes closed. "Let it in."

I was afraid. It was a beautiful thing, a glorious thing to feel myself become one with the earth, yet compared to what had happened with the crystal, this had the potential to be a tsunami, a terrifying tidal wave of energy that could fry my brain and leave me making pot holders at the state mental hospital.

"Don't worry," said Daedalus. "You will tap into only a microscopic section of the earth. You'll feel power but will be in no danger."

I hope you're right, old man, I thought, then hoped he couldn't feel my thoughts. Damn it. Had to be more careful.

"Concentrate," came Daedalus's voice, and I yanked my focus back to the spell. There was a wall of energy pressing against me. It was very different—I'd held the crystal, and its energy had been right there, blooming in my hand like a flower. This was something pressing against me from the outside.

"Let it in," Daedalus said again.

I tried to relax, to take down my natural walls. *Come on, Clio, think! Do it. You can do this. You have to do this.* I relaxed every muscle, controlling my breathing, trying to release every bit of fear or alarm I felt.

And suddenly I was flooded with light and power.

The crystal's power had been a burst within me. This was a wave washing over me, bigger, unstoppable.

"Oh," I breathed, inhaling it, feeling it fill every cell in my body. It was indescribable, an ecstatic feeling of omnipotence and joy. I felt like I could move cars with a wave of my finger or cure cancer by laying my hands on someone. I could topple bridges with my thoughts. Like the power from the crystal, it was more than intoxicating. This was why I was willing to risk feeling like death afterward, willing to destroy a crystal, willing to rip power away from the earth itself. To feel like this. I wanted to laugh.

The crystal's burst of power had lasted less than a minute. This seemed to go on and on as I took in the world around me. I glanced at a sparrow, tucked inside a shrub nearby. Instantly I became the sparrow, felt myself small and light-boned, bursting with quick-tempoed life. The world simplified in an instant, my entire existence made up of my feathers, the air moving in and out of me, the rustle of the leaves on the shrub.

Tearing myself away from the sparrow, I saw a dandelion growing in a crack in the cement. I felt its intense surge of life growing upward, felt my roots digging deeply into the thin soil for nourishment. I started crying. I felt like the goddess. I *was* the goddess.

"Yes, and now . . ." Daedalus murmured, singing softly.

"No, no, no!" I cried, snatching out at the air, at the invisible, seductive life force that I felt draining away from me, escaping into the wind, into everything around me. Within a minute it was gone. The colors of my world had drained away, leaving everything black and white. I came to, finding myself staring at Daedalus's flushed, ecstatic face, his eyes glittering. He looked younger, healthier. How long would that last?

Then I fell sideways, hitting the short grass before I'd even realized I was losing my balance. I lay sprawled awkwardly, unable to process how empty I felt, how desolate everything was without that power.

That feeling was what Melita had gone to such extreme lengths to get, including even killing her sister.

I understood why she had done it.

92

"He's asleep?" I stood on Kevin's front porch. It was a beautiful porch—shaded by huge oaks, freshly painted, and dotted with white wicker furniture. These people knew how to live.

Mr. LaTour nodded. "Yes. I'm sorry, honey. We've only just gotten home from the hospital. The doctors said he's going to need several days of total peace and quiet."

"Did they figure out what was wrong with him?" My voice was small, and I hoped the guilt wasn't written all over my face.

"No." Kevin's dad sounded worried, and I felt terrible. "It might have been some electrical aberration that won't ever happen again, but we're keeping him on a portable monitor for at least four more days. Good thing you guys don't have school next week."

"Yeah." I swallowed. "But he'll be okay?"

"He should be fine." Mr. LaTour sounded almost too hearty, and I knew he was worried—I could feel it. I was so much more in tune with people's feelings these days, since I'd gotten in touch with my magick—the magick that had almost killed my boyfriend.

"Thais—I want to thank you for what you did that day."

I looked up, eyes wide.

"I know that you steered the car away from the little girl and that you called 911 right away and stayed with Kevin until the EMTs came."

I couldn't say anything.

"The police report showed that neither of you had been drinking. I just want you to know that I was glad Kevin was with you when it happened."

Oh God. I was going to fall apart. If Kevin hadn't been with me, he would be totally fine, not on bed rest and hooked up to a heart monitor.

I nodded, trying not to cry, and pushed my small bouquet of Petra's flowers at Mr. LaTour. "If you could give him this," I said. "And this card."

He took them from me and nodded. "He'll be fine, honey," he said kindly. "And as soon as he's up to it, I know he'll want to see you."

I turned to go. The only time I was going to see Kevin again was to tell him I was breaking up with him.

Fifteen minutes later, I was walking down Daedalus's street. I'd been here only once and hoped I would recognize his door. I couldn't exactly ask anyone for his address.

I had a totally lame excuse ready—wanting to ask him about the history of the Treize, as though for a school report. All I needed was to get into his apartment for a minute, to get close to him somehow. I just prayed that he wouldn't immediately be suspicious and kick me out.

I slowed down, looking at tall, white-painted doorways. He lived close to a corner, in one of the fancy apartment buildings that bordered Jackson Square. I thought it was this one, on the north side. . . .

Tourists streamed past me, most of them watching the sidewalk artists who had set up their stands around Jackson Square. Each one had a subject perched on a stool, holding very still. I'd watched them work before, when I lived in the Quarter with Axelle. Interestingly, every one of them started a portrait by doing the person's eyes first.

Anyway. Where was it—it wasn't the one on the very corner. The second one in? An iron-gated doorway led down a short, very narrow alley to the back courtyard, where the stairs were. This had to be it.

I rang his doorbell, wiping my sweaty hands on my peasant skirt. I had rehearsed what to say a hundred times on the way down here. Minutes passed. No one leaned out over his balcony, no one buzzed me in. Just then, a woman came down the alleyway. Not even looking at me, she opened the iron gate, then held it a minute for me to go in.

"Thanks," I murmured casually, pretending to put a key back in my purse. My heart in my throat, I headed down the alleyway. Could I do this? I had come this far.

Now that I was in the courtyard, I was relieved to definitely recognize it as Daedalus's. His apartment was on the second floor—all of the apartments were, since the first floor was for stores and restaurants. I cast my senses, sending my thoughts up the stairs I was climbing, seeing if I could possibly feel Daedalus or anyone else in his apartment.

Impressions came to me from other apartments. I could tell if the occupants were male or female and what kind of energy they were putting out. It was amazing, and if I hadn't had a mission, I would have been happy to sit on the top step, close my eyes, and just see what else I could pick up.

At Daedalus's apartment I leaned against the front door, hearing nothing and feeling no presence inside. Which didn't mean anything—he could very easily cloak himself from me. Except none of them seemed to do that at home. We could always tell who was where if we were close enough. I didn't know how to cloak myself very well.

I knocked several times. No one answered. Maybe he wasn't home. Damn. I needed to do this now so I could meet with Carmela later. Just thinking about her and the ingredients she'd demanded filled me with tension and a deep sense of foreboding. Making the decision to strip Daedalus's powers from him had been my first step on this path; meeting Carmela had been the second step; and what I was doing here was the third step.

Still, this was all reversible—if I changed my mind, no harm would have been done. But eventually

I would be past the point of no return. What would that feel like?

I took a deep breath and let it out, looking at his thick front door. Okay, what to do?

It came to me in an instant: the memory of the secret room at Axelle's apartment, which had been locked. One day I'd thought about the lock opening, and I think I had actually opened it. This was before I knew I was a witch—it must have been my latent, personal magick.

This time felt different, clearer; my power seemed to flow in a clear stream from me to the lock. Within a minute I felt the tumblers fall into place, heard the faintest click of the bolt pulling back.

A door opened at the other end of the balcony, and an older couple carrying several shopping bags headed toward the stairs. Quickly I opened Daedalus's door and slipped inside, locking it behind me. I heard the couple pass, heard them bickering quietly the way old married people do.

Now, quick, quick, quick. I scanned the room and saw the door to his bedroom. This was going to be horrible, but I had the grim knowledge that this was far from the worst thing I would end up doing. I took a plastic bag out of my purse and walked through his bedroom, seeing the fastidious neatness, the beauty of the antiques, the old mirror losing its silvering, reflecting my scared face across the room.

The bathroom was through a set of narrow double doors like shutters. My heart was pounding so hard I could hear it throbbing in my ears. I tried to listen, tried to feel if anyone was coming, and got nothing. Quickly I opened drawers, looking for—

His hairbrush. This was so gross. Putting my hand inside the plastic bag, I plucked several gray hairs off the brush, then turned the bag inside out and sealed it. I stuck it in my purse, tried to set the brush in exactly the same position it had been, and carefully closed the drawers.

I was almost to the front door when I felt Daedalus coming. Was someone with him?

I froze; then instinct kicked in and I bolted into the dining room, on the other side of the living room. My first thought had been to hide under the bed, but I couldn't cross to the bedroom without being in clear sight of the front door.

Instead I crouched under the dining room table, climbing on its crossbeam and holding my skirt up tightly. I squeezed my eyes shut, realizing that Daedalus would pick up on my vibrations any second. I said all the "hide me" words that popped into my mind, but clearly this was going to end in complete disaster.

I started formulating an excuse and, better yet, an attack. The best defense is a strong offense, my dad used to say. About football.

Damn, damn, damn. *Hide me hide me hide me.*

I heard his voice in the living room, and I realized who was with him. Clio! So she had already started on her plan to increase her power. I bit my lip, feeling angry all over again. How could she do this after what he had done to me, to our father? After I'd asked her not to?

I heard books being moved around on the living room shelves.

"Here, take this," said Daedalus. "This will help paint a broader picture."

"Okay, thanks," said Clio. She sounded tired or maybe sick, and I remembered how sick she had seemed just two days ago. What had she been doing then?

"Are you all right to get home?" Daedalus asked. "Did you come down on the trolley?"

"Yeah, I'm fine," Clio said shortly. "Thanks for the stuff."

There was a pause, then Daedalus said, "I'll drive you. I didn't realize you were so affected."

"I said I'm fine," said Clio, but her voice was muffled, as if her hand were over her mouth.

"No arguments," said Daedalus, and I heard the jingle of keys. "You're ill. I'll drive you home. What you tell Petra is your business."

I heard a muffled assent, and then, unbelievably, they left! I felt them going down the stairs. Oh, I couldn't be this lucky—it seemed like even thinking about what I wanted to do would be enough bad karma to ensure that I got caught immediately.

I waited several minutes in case one of them forgot something. Finally, feeling shaky with adrenaline, I scuttled out from under the table, made sure my plastic bag was still in my purse, and slipped out the front door. My breath felt stuck in my throat, and I had literally broken out in a cold sweat, like people do in books.

I hid in the shadows of the courtyard for at least a minute, making sure the coast was clear, and then I zipped out the iron gate and lost myself in the crowds in Jackson Square. Inside the square I sat on a bench in the sun and tried to calm my shaking. It was almost half an hour before I felt like I could drive and made my way back to the rental car.

Clio, I thought, starting the car. She was really studying with Daedalus. How could she do that?

Probably the same way I could do what I was doing.

Her Face

Luc locked his car and headed up the block to Petra's house. You couldn't tell from looking that it had been in a fire, but there was still a faint scent of charred wood, burned plants, wet ash that would linger for years. It was Saturday afternoon. Would the twins be home?

Luc paused for a moment before he rang the bell. He felt Petra inside but neither twin. Both a good and a bad thing. Probably mostly good, considering his appearance. After three days of Petra's wash and mask and spell, Luc thought he noticed a slight difference. He was still a complete monster, though.

Richard was eating it up, the jerk. In general, they got along all right. But Luc knew he was everything Richard wasn't; he had things that Richard never would. Not that Richard's young face had held him back with women—Luc smiled ironically, wondering how many times Richard had pretended to lose his virginity to snag a girl.

Petra opened the door.

"I'm not sure which of us looks worse," Luc said bluntly, shocked by Petra's change.

She smiled wryly and stood back to let him in. "You do, I assure you."

Luc sighed and followed her back to the kitchen. "Yeah, I know."

"Sit down," Petra said. "Iced tea?"

"Do you have any wine?" He glanced outside—it was about two o'clock. He'd grown up drinking wine with every meal except breakfast, and it still seemed civilized.

Petra got out a bottle of red wine and poured two glasses. She didn't usually drink during the day, and Luc watched her, wondering what was up.

She sat across from him and they toasted each other silently. Petra cocked her head and examined his face, illuminated harshly by the slanting sunlight coming through the window.

"It's a little better," she said.

"A little."

"We're on the right track," Petra said. "I'll work another healing spell with you, and that will speed things up."

"Are you sure you should?"

Petra met his gaze. "The rite seems to have sapped my strength," she admitted quietly. "But magick is a muscle—if I don't use it, it will atrophy."

"What happened to you during the rite?"

"I don't know. A lot of things happened that I wasn't aware of. I was so focused on Marcel. . . ."

Luc nodded. "The lost boy."

Petra's clear gray-blue eyes looked at him. "Did you ever have sex with either of the twins?"

Luc almost spit wine all over the table. He coughed several times and wiped his mouth on his sleeve. *"What?* No! You know I didn't."

Petra just looked at him.

"Petra. You asked before, and I told you. No, things didn't get that far with either one." The memory of Thais in his arms, moaning as he kissed her deeply, touched her everywhere, rose in his mind. He shut it down, feeling the familiar sharp pain in his heart, a pain that hadn't lessened. He tried not to obviously catch his breath, to keep his face blank.

"Which one do you love?"

He frowned. "What *is* this? Look, if you don't want to work on this"—he gestured to his face—"that's fine. No problem. I appreciate what you've done so far. But what's going on?"

Letting out a breath, Petra sat back in her kitchen chair. "I don't know." She shook her head and put one hand to her cheek. "I don't know. I'm getting weird stuff—"

Luc waited, concerned. Petra was usually very calm, very centered. Right now she felt kind of ragged around the edges, unbalanced.

Finally she met his eyes again. "I don't know," she repeated. "There seem to be—plots in the air around me." She waved her hand gracefully. "I feel like things are developing, plans and schemes, like they're becoming thicker all around me. But I can't see them, can't tell exactly what they are or who they're from."

Tread carefully, Luc. "Plans and schemes? Like

what?" He felt the pressure of tension in his chest and tried to release it.

"I don't know."

"What's this have to do with me and the twins?" *Just put it out there.*

Petra didn't say anything, looking at her hands resting on the scrubbed wooden table. She took another sip of her wine. Luc waited, wondering if everything was about to be blown apart.

"Cerise was pregnant at the first rite," Petra said slowly. "If someone was trying to re-create the rite more exactly, if they really needed it to work for reasons of their own, then someone might think that a member of the Treize has to be pregnant. Only the twins are capable of getting pregnant."

"Oh, come on!" Luc scoffed. "That's crazy. Who would think that?"

Petra looked at him steadily.

Luc shook his head. "I don't know what you're feeling, Petra. I can tell you that I myself am not involved in any plan or scheme involving the twins or the Treize or whatever. My only goal right now is to fix this face."

She wouldn't try to get into his mind. Surely. They never did that to each other, or almost never. A minute slowly ticked by, measured by the almost-imperceptible creeping of the pepper shaker's shadow on the table between them.

"I don't know what I'm thinking," Petra said finally. "The twins both feel odd to me, off. I don't know what's going on." After another moment, she shook her head, as if to shake off bad feelings. "Don't listen to an old woman, Luc. It's probably nothing. I'm still trying to figure out what happened at the rite."

"Are *you* all right?"

"Yes, I'm sure I'm fine. Anyway. Let's see what we can do to speed up the healing."

Luc nodded and sat forward, waiting to do whatever Petra told him to do. Then an impression of Thais seemed to press against him, filling his arms and his heart. He caught his breath, putting a hand to his stomach to hold the feeling of her tighter.

The front door opened. Petra looked up.

"Thais," she said, and Luc's stomach tightened more. He saw her so rarely—actually, when he thought about it, he'd probably seen her fewer than fifteen times ever. Could that be possible? She was part of him, in his blood, under his skin. Every memory he had, Thais was part of. Every thought of the future contained Thais. She was still the first thing he thought of when he awoke and the last image in his mind before sleep. Luc would look at the moon's shadows moving across the walls in gray trapezoids and relive all the moments he'd had with Thais.

Of course, she hated him. Or did she? The night of the rite, he'd suddenly felt a burst of emotion from her. He'd looked up in surprise, found her eyes already shying away from him.

Now he looked like someone had thrown lye in his face.

"Hi, sweetie," said Petra. "Did you get everything you needed?"

"Yes," Thais said, moving to the counter. "I did."

Luc watched Thais set down her grocery bags. Her face was closed to him, her back stiff. He'd held her like that, her back to him, his hands curving around her stomach, pulling her to him. How had he made such a tragic mistake? How had he miscalculated so disastrously?

He knew how. He was used to getting away with everything. He'd left a thousand broken hearts behind him without losing a moment's rest over any of them. Things went his way—everything went his way. No problem had ever been so big that he couldn't just leave town over it. Ten, twenty, thirty years, things died down, people forgot. He'd gotten too sure of himself. He'd seen himself as untouchable.

And it had cost him the only person he'd ever loved, besides his sister.

And look how well that had gone.

There, she was turning around; was she going to ignore him? He felt heat rising to his scarred, ruined cheeks, felt his swollen eyelids widen as he watched her.

She put milk in the fridge, then emptied a plastic bag of apples into a basket.

"Thais—will you come join us? This healing spell would be useful to know."

Luc felt his face stiffen into an expressionless mask.

"Um, I'm supposed to go to a movie with Sylvie," Thais said, looking only at Petra.

"All right," said Petra, nodding.

Again Luc felt heat wash his face. He'd broken her heart and broken his own at the same time. Now, with the way he looked, he'd never have a chance to make it up to her, ever. She'd moved on already. He'd seen her wrapped in some kid's arms.

"How's your boyfriend?" He was as surprised as she, hearing the words.

For the first time she met his eyes. He searched her face, waiting for her to flinch at his appearance, the way everyone did on the street. But she showed no reaction.

"He's fine," she said shortly. "We're breaking up." Immediately she frowned: she hadn't meant to say that.

His brilliant flare of hope was instantly extinguished by the knowledge of what he looked like. He had no hope of this pain being eased, and he looked down at the table.

"I won't be late," Thais told Petra; then she turned and left the kitchen.

"All right, honey," said Petra. "Be careful."

"Okay."

He heard her run lightly upstairs, imagined the way her full, colorful skirt would swirl around her legs. She was down again in a minute; then all that was left was the fresh lavender scent of her hair and the echo of the front door closing.

Slowly he let out a deep breath, as if that would ease the pain. His eyes met Petra's. "Can we do the spell?"

Perhaps Thais

Clio was an apt pupil, Daedalus thought again, entering his apartment. True, she was affected badly by the magick they'd made—but that would lessen in time. It was like anything else: one became inured to it. One developed calluses.

But really, she was gifted. He had to show her something only once, and she remembered it with certainty the next time. It was very gratifying.

And she seemed grateful for his lessons—she had a goal and, like himself, was single-minded in her pursuit of it. It was a quality he admired. The twins, more than anyone of Cerise's line, seemed to embody the old spirit of the time they sprang from, in their looks as well as their strength.

He couldn't kill Clio to make room for Melita. It would have to be someone else. Someone had to go, and Daedalus was biding his time, waiting patiently to make the best decision. Should he kill the weakest? That would be Sophie. The one most likely to betray him? That was harder to discern. Petra? Jules? Not Jules, not after all these years. But he could do the most damage if he did betray Daedalus. Jules was above reproach, though, Daedalus was sure of it.

Daedalus moved to the kitchen and poured himself a glass of *eau gazeuse* with a twist of lime. Clio was very strong—she'd been in his apartment only a few minutes, yet he imagined he could still pick up her vibrations, barely perceptible but there.

Perhaps Thais should be the one to die. She wasn't on his side; he could feel it. She could become quite a liability, with her unusual strength and lack of respect for his position. He would have to ponder this.

He paused halfway through the living room. Axelle. What did she want? He sighed, moving to turn on the ceiling fan. Axelle could be extremely tiresome sometimes. But useful too, he admitted. Better to be gracious and keep on her good side.

He opened the door just as she reached up to knock.

"My dear," he said, ushering her inside. "I've been thinking about you. No ill effects from the rite, then?"

"No," she said. "But you look like hell."

Trust Axelle to point out the elephant in the room.

"Do I?" Daedalus said smoothly, moving to open the tall French windows that led to the street-side balcony. He held his shoulders back and moved with firm strides.

"Yes, you do," she said, reclining on one of his Empire settees. "Rough night?"

And just then, a thought crept into his head, the dim recognition of something he'd been missing. Since the rite, he'd been weaker. And so had Petra, he'd heard. The two of them, the most powerful witches in the Treize—aside, of course, from Melita—suddenly struggling for energy. It only followed that someone had taken their power at that rite. Someone had used the rite to draw in more magick, and that magick had to come from somewhere.

It had come from himself and Petra, and it had been taken by . . .

Axelle.

Daedalus smiled at Axelle patronizingly, carefully blocking his thoughts from her. "Is there something I can help you with?" He sat across from her and set his water on a silver coaster. Now wasn't the time to share what he knew. He would wait, and he would find the right way to repay her.

"Yes," Axelle said, crossing her long legs and putting her red-painted toes up on the settee's arm, which was obviously calculated to annoy him. "Let's get Melita home."

Thaïs

It wasn't any easier going back to Mama Loup's now that I knew the way. The neighborhood seemed even more threatening, and though it was daytime, the light around Mama Loup's house seemed dimmer and the air heavier. I parked the rental as close as I could, said spells of protection around it, and tried to look brave and untouchable as I passed people sitting on their stoops, dogs barking at their chain-link fences, kids racing by on too-small bikes.

I went through the rusty iron gate and headed around the side, an old pro. The alley was barely two feet wide, and wild vines covered the thin bamboo fence. This house, like ours, like most houses in New Orleans, was raised up several feet on brick pillars. I could smell the damp soil from beneath the house and had no desire to see what else might be under there.

The same bare-bulb fixture was lit above the same broken screen door. Again, the wooden inside door was open. I pulled open the screen and stepped into the dark interior. After the daylight, blinking made things look polarized and orange. I stood still, wishing my eyes would adjust faster.

There were other people in the shop—the same woman who had waited on me before, who I thought was Mama Loup. She was talking seriously with another woman who looked thin and strung out. A plump baby sat on her hip, clinging to her T-shirt with small, wet fists.

I wandered over by the counter, not wanting to interrupt them, hoping Carmela would see me and come out. Old metal shelves made short aisles in the room, and I started looking at dusty glass bottles with handwritten labels and plastic bags sealed with twist ties. One bag contained what looked like several dried green lizards, and I tried not to grimace.

"That'll make him come back to you for true," I heard Mama Loup murmur. "You rub that *perlain-pain* on anything he wears, he can't help but come back to you, no."

A love spell. I'd gotten the impression, from Clio and Petra, that to stoop to such a thing was embarrassing, humiliating. I remembered Luc in my room at Axelle's, angry, saying, "I could make you love me." Luc.

I didn't hate him. I was still angry, furious, at what he had done. But I couldn't seem to muster up hatred. Now, looking at him, he was so different— his natural confidence, almost arrogance, had been obliterated along with his handsome face. He seemed humbled. That could only be a good thing, I thought meanly, then turned as I heard someone come through the hanging bamboo beads that curtained a dark doorway.

It was Carmela, I knew, but once again she seemed to carry her own personal storm cloud with her, making her harder to see, to distinguish.

"You're back, child," she said. "I said not to come back until—"

"I have everything on the list," I interrupted her. Her dark eyes blinked once, which I took to indicate surprise.

"Everything?"

"Yes." I patted the canvas carryall I had on my shoulder.

For several moments she gazed at me, and looking back at her, I saw only her eyes, as black as Axelle's.

"Then come this way." She held the beaded curtain aside with one hand. My heart in my throat, I stepped around the back of the counter, passed her, and entered the black room beyond.

It was a hallway, short and unlit, like a cave, and I could see only the barest outline of a doorway on the left. Feeling slightly hysterical, it occurred to me that this warren of rooms was like the magick tent in Harry Potter—small and normal on the outside, but going on and on for an impossible distance on the inside. Already it seemed like there was no way all these rooms could be contained in the small house I had entered.

"In here." In this room there was more than just

113

an absence of light—the walls seemed to actually deaden light. The idea of warmth and sunlight outside seemed like a distant memory.

My throat was dry—I couldn't swallow. I felt hyper-alert, as if going through a carnival fun house, on guard against anything that might spring out at me. But the truth was, I had put myself in a dangerous situation, and if things went south, I probably wouldn't be able to save myself.

And I was so glad I'd just had that thought. *Put it out of your mind.*

"Show me what you have."

I blinked at Carmela's voice, my eyes widening to let in as much light as possible. There was a faint scratch, then a match flared into a swaying dance, and I saw Carmela's tan hand lighting black candles, three of them, held in a twisted silver candelabra.

Now I saw a small table, saw that we were in a room maybe nine feet square. The walls weren't painted black, as I'd thought—they were a dark, oxblood red. Out of nowhere I flashed on the fact that on wooden warships, in the olden days, the doctor's little room for surgery had been painted red so the men couldn't see all the blood and get scared.

Great. Thank you for that.

I tried again to swallow, unsuccessfully, then started pulling things out of my bag. Three forked twigs from a weeping willow. Red clay dust made by rubbing an old brick on the sidewalk. Little pieces of unworked silver that I'd bought at Botanika. A hard cone of pressed brown sugar I'd gotten from a bodega on Magazine Street. The plastic bag with Daedalus's hair. Some powdered sassafras leaves from Botanika.

I laid everything out. Carmela examined it all.

"What's this stuff for?" I asked.

She looked up at me, eyes glowing like a cat's. "The silver is because I'm making a necklace and thought it would look pretty. The brown sugar is good in coffee—you scrape it with your spoon. The sassafras is called filé, and you sprinkle it on gumbo to thicken it right before you eat it. The brick dust is useful for different spells, and the willow twigs were just for fun, to see if you would bother finding them."

I stared at her.

"But this, this is very interesting," she said, picking up the plastic bag containing a few silver hairs. "I didn't think you would get this, child." She looked at me appraisingly, as if this one ingredient made her take me seriously.

"Tell me more about what you want to do." Her English was fine grammatically, but she had an accent that didn't seem quite French or quite anything else.

"I want revenge," I managed to get out. "This witch, the man whose powers I want to strip—he killed my father with magick. I can't kill him, but I could take his powers away. If you help me."

"Why can't you kill him?" Oddly, in this bare room, her words had no echo but fell from her lips

115

like stones falling silently into still water, leaving no ripple.

Because he's immortal?

"He's a murderer," I said. "I'm not."

"Being stripped of power would be worse for any witch," Carmela said thoughtfully.

"Yes." *Even for me?* I wondered.

"Do you have any idea what stripping a witch's powers is like?"

No. "I think it would be really bad but that it wouldn't kill him."

"I'll show you, on something smaller," she said, pushing back the full sleeves of her caftan. Like Mama Loup, she wore a long, African-print robe and a matching turban. "And then you will decide."

"Okay." This didn't sound so bad. Unless . . . "You don't mean, like, an animal, do you?"

Carmela paused and turned toward me. "Would that bother you, Thais? Surely an animal is less than a human being?"

"Animals are . . . innocent," I said, tension winding around my spine like wire. "People aren't."

She looked at me consideringly. "Surely some people are?" It sounded rhetorical.

I thought about my dad, who had lied to me about my being a twin. I thought of Clio, who was studying with my mortal enemy behind my back. I thought of Luc, who had betrayed me. And Petra, who had lied to Clio for seventeen years. It was inextricably part of being human, I thought sadly.

116

People lied, cheated, hurt the ones they loved. "No," I said. "No one."

She laughed, showing small white teeth. "So young to be such a cynic. So very young."

"I'm more of a realist," I said.

"Not an animal, then," said Carmela, in a tone that made me think she'd never planned to use an animal anyway. She reached beneath the table and took out a potted plant, a perfect long-stemmed orchid. Totally anticlimactic.

I blinked. It was a potted plant—its roots weren't even in the earth. What power could it have?

"Come." Carmela walked past the table to where a silver circle was painted on the floor. All around the circle were painted small runes and other symbols I didn't recognize. It was weird—as soon as I stepped into it, it was like stepping into a . . . well, to call it a windstorm is too dramatic. Not a tornado. But like a faint vortex of some kind, held solely within this dinky painted circle in this little back room of a house in New Orleans. I definitely felt it, like a fan beneath the floor, pulling at my skirt. It was so weird.

"Sit," said Carmela, gesturing to the floor. She sat down across from me and put the plant between us. "Everything has power, magickal power," she went on. "And a life force. Those two things overlap, and in some cases they overlap completely, inseparable. The thing is, if you take something's life force, you also take its magickal power. But sometimes you can take something's power,

117

but not its life force. You can do that with people. And most animals. And some plants."

"Okay," I said, feeling my palms get sweaty on my knees.

"Now . . ."

The beginning of her spell was familiar in that we centered ourselves, as though for meditation. Then Carmela began singing in a chanting, singsong kind of way, like I'd heard others do. Then, with no warning, I was sucked into the spell, pinned motionless by what was happening, and could only sit and watch.

Carmela's spell was like turning a black light onto a black-light poster, where unseen colors suddenly popped and the whole thing looked different. One minute I was looking at an orchid in a pot, and the next I was looking at an alien, vibrating thing, practically glowing with a faint green light, visibly radiating energy or power or whatever it was.

"This is its life," Carmela said softly, stroking her tan fingers along one glowing-edged leaf. "And this is its magick." She gestured to the plant, how it seemed to be spiky with movement, vibrating like a plucked string. "We leave its life but strip its magick. We're not going to take its magick for ourselves. This time."

She began to sing again, and I recognized about every tenth word as sounding French.

She moved her hands over the plant, and I swore I could see a dim outline of the plant slowly untwine itself from the actual plant. It was like a thin, shimmering blue-green line, orchid-shaped, and Carmela's hands seemed to coax it away. I was frozen in place, eyes wide, wondering if I were hallucinating. Clearly this was magick on a different scale, and with a far different intent, than anything I'd been exposed to.

I felt the outline's small, fluttery vibrations, like a butterfly's wings brushing against me. Carmela seemed to gather it in her palm, then opened her fingers in a starburst shape. The outline coiled and then broke apart, a silent firecracker shattering into thousands of tiny shards. They arched and fell but dissipated almost instantly, and I felt nothing fall around me.

"Oh my God," I whispered, awed. "That was amazing. That was its power, its magick?"

Carmela nodded seriously, then gestured down at the orchid.

I sucked in my breath, recoiling instinctively.

The orchid was . . . not dead. Still alive, it drooped in its pot, but I had the shocking feeling that it was obscene somehow, something grotesque and perverse. I blinked a couple of times, trying to figure out what I was seeing.

It was . . . an orchid, in a pot. It drooped visibly, and its colors were definitely duller, faded. But besides that, there was something about it that filled me with revulsion, that felt awful and horrifying, like I'd stumbled on a rotting corpse in a wood.

"What's . . . wrong with it?" I managed to get out.

"We stripped it of its magick. Like you want to do to your witch."

"It's not dead?"

"No. It won't live long, but it's not dead."

"Why does it feel so awful?" I could barely speak; my eyes were riveted to the plant.

"Because it has no magick."

I met her dark eyes, confused.

"Magick is what makes life worth living," she said matter-of-factly. "This has no magick."

I stared again at the plant, how it seemed so repugnant to me, worse than dead.

"And this will happen to Daedalus? The witch?"

Carmela's eyes flashed. She seemed to look right through my pupils to my soul itself. "Yes."

I swallowed, feeling like I might be sick. "Good," I whispered.

Clio

"What?" Nan looked shocked, and two spots of heat appeared on her cheeks.

I scraped my plate into the garbage and picked up Thais's. Neither of us had eaten much dinner, but I didn't think I would be sick. The herbs and spell that Daedalus had given me earlier had helped a lot, and I was acting pretty normal. As opposed to Thais, who had slept all afternoon after some strenuous shoe shopping.

"Here." Thais put our three glasses on the counter, then took a dishcloth to wipe down the table. She'd been acting weird since yesterday—cold, not looking at me or talking to me. I hadn't had a chance to ask her what was up.

"I said, *what*?" Nan was looking at me in horror.

I'd known this conversation was going to be really hard, but it had been on my mind, and I wanted to get it over with. Since Nan had just told me to call Melysa to set up a time to study for my ROA, this seemed like a good moment.

"I don't want to do my rite of ascension," I repeated. "At least, not right now."

"Clio—you're going to be eighteen next month." Nan left the trash where it was and folded her arms, looking at me.

"I know. But with everything that's been going on—the Treize, the rite, everything—it's impossible for me to focus on it," I explained. "Maybe next year, when things have settled down."

"No, not next year!" Nan exclaimed. "*This* year, next month, like we planned."

"Plus I think it would be great if Thais and I did it together."

Thais snorted over by the table.

"Thais won't be ready for her ROA for maybe five or six years," Nan said. "And you know it."

"Well—" There was something else that I wasn't telling her. Usually, in our religion, a witch made her rite of ascension as both a test and a tool to help her solidify her strengths and knowledge. I didn't need to do that. Right now I couldn't see how it would help me feel more centered in my power. I was studying with Daedalus, learning a lot, and I already knew I was more powerful than any other witch in Nan's *cercle*, besides her. The witches of the Treize were all so much more powerful than ordinary witches, and it looked like that power had been handed down to me and Thais.

I just couldn't see the point.

"Clio, you've been working toward this for a long time," said Nan, leaning over and tying the top of the trash bag.

"I know. I don't want to disappoint anyone," I

said. I scrubbed a plate with soapy water and rinsed it. "But I've got too much going on. You have to admit, the last month has been a roller coaster. There's no way I can focus on the ROA."

"The party has been planned."

I looked at her. "No, it hasn't," I said, smiling. "You know you haven't gotten that far with it."

Nan pressed her lips together, clearly thinking, *Smartass.*

"Look, I'll do it later," I said, thinking that I wasn't really lying. "But goddess, Nan—I've had so many huge things explode in my life lately. I can't take one more pressure."

"No, I can't allow you to throw this away so easily," Nan said crossly. "You've been studying for a long time, and I won't have you waste it."

"Knowledge is never wasted," I said, keeping a lid on my temper. "*You* said that."

"Look, you're going to make your rite of ascension next month, and that's final."

I didn't say anything but dried my hands on a dish towel. There wasn't any point to arguing more. Later I would probably have to dig my heels in again, but for now I was going to drop it. I looked up to see Thais watching us, and I was sure she was happy to be out of it.

"What are you doing tonight?" I asked her. "How's the Kevster?"

After a quick, startled glance at the change in topic, she looked away from me, her face guarded. "Fine."

I wasn't positive she needed to break up with him myself. Maybe this was why she was acting weird. No—it seemed to be about me in particular.

"I'm going to meet Racey downtown," I said. "Want to come with?"

For a moment she paused, as if considering, then gave me a cool look and shook her head. "I've got a killer headache," she said. "Maybe it's allergies. I'm going to stay in and go to bed early."

"Okaaay." We couldn't have it out in front of Nan, but if she wanted to be that way, fine. I draped the dish towel over the sink to dry, and when I glanced up, Nan was giving me an eagle-eyed look.

"What?" I said.

"This discussion is not over," she said.

I sighed. "Please just think about where I'm coming from. But right now I'm going to meet Racey." I prayed that she wouldn't suddenly put her foot down and say I couldn't go. I wasn't up for a big battle.

I saw the thought processes going on in her head. Finally she nodded shortly. "We'll talk about this later. Don't be out too late."

I nodded. "Okay. Hope you feel better, Thais."

"Yeah, thanks."

Then I grabbed my purse and car keys, and I was gone.

In the car, I pulled out my phone and dialed Racey's number. At the last second, I didn't hit send. I steered with one hand, holding my phone in the other, and thought about where my head was. What did I feel like doing? Who did I feel like being with?

No one. Someone new and fabulous.

With irritation I remembered how Richard had grabbed me the other day, when Nan had been working on Luc. No one had ever pissed me off as regularly as Richard did. If only I could wipe that smirk off his face once and for all.

And Luc. Goddess, what had happened to him? I really did think it was a shame, but it also seemed to be a living example of the threefold law. He'd put some bad energy out into the world, some real pain, and what do you know, he'd gotten the same back.

I was amazed at how resigned he was too, how incredibly horrible he looked, after looking like a god on earth for so long. He seemed to accept it as his fate—he wasn't raging against it or saying it was unfair. To me that meant he understood that what he'd done had been wrong and bad and that he should pay for it.

My thoughts exactly.

But I did feel sorry for him. Nan had said that he felt like a leper, walking around town. That people actually gasped and turned away. That had to suck. If that had happened to me, I'd be hiding under my bedcovers for the rest of my life or until it got fixed somehow. At least Nan had mentioned that his face was improving a bit.

Looking up, I saw I was already at Jackson Avenue, halfway downtown. Maybe . . . maybe I would go see Luc. See how he was. He didn't deserve my help, and I wouldn't offer it. Still, if everyone was freaking out when they saw him, it would be nice for him to see someone who could deal with his face the way it was.

Richard answered the door, unfortunately. He was in his standard uniform of unbuttoned plaid flannel shirt, ratty jeans, and bare feet. His sun-streaked hair looked like he'd just gotten out of bed. I'd been taking extra care with my appearance to cheer myself up, and I looked hot in a gauzy peasant shirt you could see my bra through and a pair of tight capris that stopped just below my knees.

It was nighttime, but the Quarter was well lit, and I was standing practically under a streetlamp. I frowned up at him, and something hit me—he looked different, but how? I couldn't put my finger on it.

"I was hoping you were out," I said bluntly.

"You're out of luck," he said. "What's up? Selling something door-to-door?" He looked me up and down with a mocking gaze, making it clear what he thought I should be selling. Bastard.

"Here to see Luc," I said, crossing my arms over my chest.

"Should I frisk you for weapons?"

I tried not to shiver at the thought of his hands patting me down. Instead I smiled sarcastically and didn't answer. He stepped back from the door and made a sweeping motion with one hand, waving me inside.

I walked through the doorway, careful not to touch him, but as I passed, I smelled his detergent, the scent of cigarette smoke, and . . . some kind of spice? Unmistakably Richard. I knew it very well.

He inhaled as I passed, and from the corner of my eye I saw the smooth tan skin over his collarbones, saw the beginnings of his tribal tattoos. Keeping my eyes straight forward, I went down the hall to Luc's room, which I'd never been in. Ironically enough.

Their apartment was a typical half of a double: the front door opened into a long hall that had a row of rooms on the right-hand side. First was a living room, which I'd never paid attention to. I didn't even know if it had furniture. Then Richard's room, with its single mattress on the floor. Then Luc's room. At the end of the hall was the bathroom, and the last room was on the left in a stuck-on addition, making a T: the kitchen. The ceilings were at least twelve feet high, the floor moldings maybe fourteen inches. Two small brass chandeliers, one at each end of the hallway, cast inadequate light. It would be beautiful if someone with money bought it and redid it.

"I'll leave you to it, then," Richard said behind me, and I heard the door to his room shut. I knew it had to be burning him that I was here to see Luc and not him.

Tough.

I knocked on Luc's door. He must know I was here, from my voice if not my vibes.

"Let me in," I said. It was then that I realized he wasn't alone—I felt a female presence. My jaw dropped, and without thinking I turned the doorknob and pushed.

Luc sat on the side of an antique sleigh bed. His arms were around a girl who was covering her face, clearly sobbing. I stood there, dumbstruck, thinking, *My God, even with that face he's getting girls.* Then she looked up, and I was struck again: it was *Sophie,* and she looked like hell. I knew that she and Manon had broken up, that Manon had moved to Axelle's—but here she was on Luc's *bed,* with his arms around her. Was he taking advantage of her wrecked emotional state to get somewhere with her?

I gave him an icy glare.

"Clio!" he said, clearly surprised.

"Never mind," I said, stepping back and pulling the door shut hard. My face burned and I was furious at him all over again.

"Clio, wait!" he called through the door.

Sophie sobbed again, and Luc said something to her. But I was already striding down the hallway, incensed, reaching for my phone to call Racey to meet me at Amadeo's.

Predictably, Richard's door opened, spilling a rectangle of warm light into the hallway, and I whirled on him.

"Get a good laugh out of that?" I hissed. "You knew he wasn't alone!"

He pretended not to know what I meant, looking confused. "No, Sophie's in there."

"No fricking duh!" I said. "Thanks, jerk!" I spun away and headed for the front door. Richard caught up to me, and since he never had a problem putting his hands all over me, he grabbed my arm. I stopped with a jolt.

"What did *I* do?" he demanded. "I didn't make her go in there. And it's just Sophie."

" 'Just Sophie,' " I mimicked. "And they're on his bed, and his arms are around her!"

Richard looked at me oddly. "Well, we *are* in the South."

I stared at him, having no idea what he was talking about. Was he saying that being in the South makes people act crazy from the heat? Makes them hornier? I shook my head and tried to yank free, but instead he dragged me into the living room.

It was dark and unfurnished, because Luc and Richard were perhaps the two least-domestic guys I'd ever met. The long French windows overlooking the street were shuttered, but their transoms let in the streetlamp's light, so I could see Richard's face.

He pushed the door shut with one foot, keeping hold of me.

"Let go of me!" I hissed.

"Why are you so mad at *me?*" he said, his eyes watching my mouth.

My eyes widened. "Where should I *start?*" I pulled my arm one last time, and he let me go but stood between me and the door, looking like he wasn't going to move.

"How long are you going to be mad about that?

Ballpark figure?" he said irritably, and I assumed he was talking about the whole "attempted murder" wrinkle.

"Um, *forever*?" I'd never had a crush on Richard, never needed to win him over, so I'd never tempered my anger or watched my words or tried to pretty things up. I always let him have it with both barrels. And he always took it. And came back for more. Come to think of it, he was the only guy I spoke totally straight with, all the time. Basically, it probably confirmed his opinion of me as a total bitch.

In the next second, just like that, it was like he'd flicked a switch and gone from regular annoying Richard to deadly seductive Richard. Eyes staying focused on my mouth, he stepped a bit closer and visibly let go of his irritation and impatience.

Oh no, I thought, backing up. *No.*

"No, not forever," he murmured, his voice silky.

"Leave me alone," I said.

He never listened to me. His hand reached out and curled around the back of my neck. I stiffened, narrowing my eyes at him in a way that had once made someone cry.

"Clio," he said, so close that I could feel the heat of his skin. "We don't like each other. But we have this between us. If we gave in to it, maybe it would go away."

Yes, said my stupid, easily convinced body.

"No. Don't be an ass," I said.

I braced myself as he leaned closer, tilting his head to kiss my neck. I pulled back, but he pursued me, pressing his lips against my skin. Again I had an odd, vague sense that something was just slightly . . . different. It made me crazy not being able to put my finger on it. His mouth was warm and firm and familiar, and shivers ran down my spine. I instantly felt my knees start to melt, which pissed me off. He left another kiss on my neck, by my collarbone, and my heart sped up and my breath got shallow. He always did this—the Richard effect.

"No, go *away*," I said crossly, and pushed against his hard shoulders. Then my hands slid over his shirt, feeling his heat through the cloth, and my brain went dead. He pulled me to him, one hand against the small of my back, one hand sliding up my side. His stomach seemed to burn me through my thin shirt, and all I could think was, *Uhhhh . . .* Slowly, slowly, he kissed his way up my neck and across my cheek while my eyelids fluttered closed.

Somehow, when he kissed me, everything else went away—my pain over Luc, my fear and dread about working with Daedalus, Nan, Thais being upset with me—it all faded. All I was aware of was Richard's scent, how he felt, how his hands felt moving over me.

Just as his mouth covered mine, I heard Luc's door opening and footsteps coming down the hall. My eyes flew open and I quickly stepped back.

"Damn it!" Richard said, reaching for me, but I had my sanity again and dodged around him, lunging for the living room door, opening it.

Sophie, still looking upset but no longer crying,

nodded at me. "Clio," she said, as if it were no big deal that I'd found her in Luc's bedroom. After all, they'd known each other for two hundred years; who knew if they'd been lovers before she'd gotten together with Manon? She opened the front door and left, with one last look at Luc.

I almost choked when I saw how he looked back at her—I actually saw the love in his eyes, the only part of his ruined face capable of expressing emotion.

The front door closed, and Luc looked at me. Then he looked at Richard, standing close behind me, and saw that we had just come out of the living room. He frowned, looking back and forth. I could hear Richard breathing hard.

"What's going on?" Luc said.

"Nothing," I said shortly, heading for the front door. Once again, I was disgusted with both of them and with guys in general.

"You two—what's going *on*?" Luc said, but this time I heard comprehension in his voice.

"Nothing. You're the one with the girl in your room." I reached the front door and pulled it open.

"What?" Luc asked, sounding incredulous. Little Mr. Innocent. "That was *Sophie!*"

"Uh-huh." I stormed outside and slammed their door behind me. Damn both of them! And damn *me*, for giving in to Richard *again*.

The door opened and Richard came out as I stomped down the steps.

"We have to sort this out," he said in a low voice, gesturing between himself and me.

"No, we don't," I said, and began to head to my car.

"Clio!" Luc's voice. Disbelieving, I turned around.

"What are you doing with Richard?" He sounded almost outraged, which was a big laugh and pushed me over the edge. I was so mad at both of them and even more mad at myself that I just lashed out stupidly.

"I'm *sleeping* with him!" I snapped, and then felt worse than mortified when a passerby turned because she'd heard me. My cheeks flamed and I wanted to scream.

Luc's jaw dropped open and Richard started in surprise, then grinned lopsidedly.

I pressed my lips together so I wouldn't start shrieking swearwords at the top of my lungs. Shaking my head, keeping my mouth shut tight, I whirled and practically ran down the sidewalk.

"Oh, Clio!" Richard called after me. I ignored him. "Sophie is Luc's *sister!*"

Stupid Idiot

Luc came back inside and shut the door hard, glaring at Richard.

Richard just grinned and headed for the kitchen.

"She's lying," Luc said, following him.

"Yep, uh-huh," Richard replied in a tone calculated to make Luc insane. He flicked on the kitchen light and got a glass out of a cupboard.

"She's totally lying," Luc said. "You didn't get in her pants."

Richard poured himself half a tumbler of whiskey and took a sip, looking innocent. This was too good. He would have to thank Clio later for giving him the most fun he'd had in weeks.

"Admit it," Luc demanded, his hands on his hips.

"Why do you care? I thought you were hot for Thais."

Luc started to look angry. "Tell me she's lying."

"I'm not going to tell you anything," said Richard, brushing past him.

"Listen, you stay away from her."

He really sounded mad, which was verrry interesting. Richard knew Clio still had warped feelings for Luc, but he'd thought Luc was resigned to his disgraced status. The two of them pissed him off—Clio for still thinking she loved Luc when clearly she was all wrapped up in Richard, and Luc for being the greedy bastard that he was. He couldn't have either twin, but he didn't want Richard to have Clio either.

Which was too bad.

Because Richard was coming to terms with the fact that he did want her.

Really, really wanted her.

"What's it to you?" Richard asked, leaning against the door frame, drinking his whiskey.

"You stay away from her," Luc repeated, actually pointing his finger at Richard. "She loves me, and I love her."

Richard laughed. "No, you don't."

"Yes, I do," Luc insisted.

Richard shook his head in disgust. "Whatever. May the best man win."

"You're not even in the running!" Luc almost shouted. "You're her frigging grandfather!"

Richard stared at him. "What the hell are you talking about?"

"Clio and Thais are the thirteenth generation of Cerise's line," Luc said deliberately. "Where did Cerise's line come from?"

Right. Richard had fathered Cerise's baby, and he felt the familiar barbed-wire feeling in his heart at the memory of it. Thirteen generations later, the baby he had made had descendents, Clio and Thais.

Yes, he *was* related to them. But incredibly, incredibly distantly. The connection certainly wasn't close to significant by now.

"I'm not their grandfather," Richard said. "The percentage I'm related to them is so small I can't even figure it out."

"You're still related! I'm telling you, Richard, don't touch her."

"Why not, Luc?" Richard made his voice mild, but he knew that Luc knew him so well that this should be a sign for caution, if not outright alarm.

"She's mine."

Richard's eyes narrowed. "Really. Does she know that? Is that why she can't keep her hands off me?"

Luc looked stunned, then quickly recovered. He stalked back to his own room, shaking his head. "You're lying."

"Yeah," said Richard, raising his voice so Luc couldn't help hearing him. "She and I are *both* lying."

Luc slammed his door.

Richard swirled his drink in his glass, then set the glass down. He had to go get something to eat.

If He Had Loved Her

"Smells and bells," they called it, the "high Church" style of service. A typical Sunday in a town still very Catholic. The priests swung the heavy brass censer, and they carried the Bible around the church, doing the stations of the cross. It was beautiful, ultimately civilized and yet very primitive at the same time.

Everyone stood, and Marcel stood also. He had this rear pew almost to himself—only an old woman shared the very far end. A strand of jet beads, her rosary, dangled from one hand. Automatically Marcel tapped his pockets, but the plain wooden beads he'd once carried everywhere were no longer tucked into his monk's robe.

It was time for the sermon, and the priest ascended into the pulpit and turned on the microphone. Marcel sighed, wishing for the churches of a hundred years ago, a hundred and fifty. As the priest began to talk about how they, as ordinary people, could embody the reflection of Christ in everyday living, Marcel let his mind wander.

Axelle, Claire, and Sophie.

Three women he now unexpectedly found himself in relationships with. Three women he doubted he'd spoken to more than a dozen times in two hundred years. Axelle was still self-serving and duplicitous but also unexpectedly shrewd and generous. Claire he'd written off when she was fifteen and already had a reputation as a loose skirt. God knew she'd only gone downhill from there—with each new age of civilization, it seemed she found new opportunities for depravity. Now she seemed—fun-loving and lovelorn. She was in love with Jules. Now that he finally recognized it, Marcel, looking back, couldn't remember a time when Claire had not apparently been in love with Jules.

And Jules wouldn't give in to her, for some reason. Why? Marcel saw love in his eyes as well. What was holding Jules back? Now, at last, Marcel could see, if you loved someone for hundreds of years and they didn't love you back, you might very well want to try every diversion you could to take your mind off it. When he looked at it that way, it was much easier to empathize with Claire and even admire her courage.

And then . . . Sophie. Long, long ago, Sophie had loved him, had pined for him. And he'd never seen it. He'd focused his sights on one person— Cerise—and had never looked to either side.

People around him stood again, and Marcel mindlessly began singing the closing hymn. The priest in his white robe and embroidered alb passed, palms locked together in prayer as he sang. Everyone filed out after him: deacon, altar boys, choir.

Sophie had been a lovely girl. Marcel grimaced—clearly, she was lovely still. How long had she pined for him before giving up? How many shy signals, glances, slight overtures had she made toward him that he hadn't noticed?

Almost groaning, Marcel rubbed his temples and waited to exit his pew.

Sophie. He had missed out.

Marcel went out into a humid, too-warm Sunday afternoon. It was thickly overcast, and the breeze carried the scent of rain. He wandered aimlessly onto the wide slate flagstones that bordered Jackson Square.

Sophie was beautiful, in a quiet, deeply feminine way. She was one of the few truly nice people he'd ever known, someone truly without avarice or meanness or anger.

What would his life have been like if he'd loved Sophie instead of Cerise? He could have been loved instead of given a number and been squeezed in whenever Richard wasn't in her bed.

Acid burned his stomach, and he forced himself to control his anger. It had all been so long ago. Richard had been just a kid. Only recently had Marcel actually realized that. Richard had been only fifteen. Cerise had been four years older—she should have known better. In a way, she'd taken advantage of Richard. And Marcel too, both of them. Gotten what she wanted without giving either of them what they'd wanted.

Marcel found himself on the corner of St. Ann and Chartres.

Sophie and Manon had broken up—possibly for good.

Marcel turned and headed deeper into the Quarter. Maybe Axelle would want to get some lunch somewhere. Or Claire and Jules.

Marcel's mouth quirked in a slightly surprised smile. He had friends.

WWCD?

"Marcel, huh? I have to admit, I missed that one." Claire handed Sophie a Snickers bar, then lay down on Jules's pink futon sofa. She ripped open the end of her own Snickers and took a bite.

Sophie nodded miserably and looked at the candy bar as if needing instructions.

"Just eat it, honey," said Claire, chewing.

Looking like she had nothing to lose, Sophie carefully undid the wrapper and took a tentative bite. Claire tried hard not to roll her eyes. It was a frigging Snickers bar, for God's sake. What rock had Sophie been living under?

Jules hadn't had any Kleenex, so a roll of toilet paper sat next to Sophie's chair, along with a paper grocery bag of used tissue.

"I never wanted anyone to know," Sophie said. Her voice was thick with chocolate and crying. "I only told Manon because—" She sniffled again and took another bite of peanuty goodness. "I told her after we became . . . friends, years after the rite."

"Hmm." Claire carefully scratched her nose next to her silver nose ring. "Well, Marcel knows now.

The question—well, one of the questions—is, are you and Manon going to patch things up?"

Sophie looked stricken, her face gaunt and pale. "I don't know," she whispered. She shook her head and bit off more Snickers. "I thought for sure we would— we always do. But now I don't know. Manon says she'll never forgive me."

"Yeah," Claire said quickly, wanting to steer the conversation to a less weepy topic. "But if you don't get back with Manon, how about hooking up with Marcel? God knows he's still single."

Sophie looked struck by the thought. Had it not occurred to her? Maybe Claire should hand over the "dense" award.

"I don't know," Sophie said, seeming lost. "But he doesn't care about me—he doesn't know I'm alive."

"He does now," Claire assured her.

"And—he took a vow of celibacy when he became a monk," Sophie went on. "I remember hearing that."

Claire rolled her eyes. "He's a guy."

"And I still love Manon," Sophie said, her voice wavering.

Sitting up, Claire balled her candy bar wrapper and threw it across the small room into Sophie's tissue bag. "Okay, so you still love her. She'd be a hard habit to break. But if she's ready to move on, then you have no choice but to move on too. And if you don't want a regular guy, one with a short life span, then Marcel might be the way to go."

"I can't even think about it now," said Sophie, brushing her long dark hair off her face.

"Well, plenty of time," Claire said, making a massive understatement. "The thing about unrequited love is that it doesn't tend to go away."

She felt Sophie looking at her and hoped her voice hadn't sounded really bitter.

"Where's Jules?" Sophie asked, following Claire's train of thought.

"He got a job," Claire said. "Inexplicably."

Claire looked at her bright red toenails, mulling over the surprising fact that she and Sophie the Ice Maiden actually had something in common these days.

"Have you ever been with a guy?" she asked.

Sophie blushed. "No. When I was younger— well, it wasn't done." Then she seemed to remember that Claire had in fact done it quite a bit, with boys and men in their village. She hurried on. "I just couldn't—with my parents watching me all the time. Then I was in love with Marcel, for a long, long time. When he disappeared after the rite, I wondered if he was with Melita—if he'd run away with her, if they were lovers. Maybe he'd loved them both."

"I doubt it," said Claire.

"But he was gone. So even though Cerise was . . . dead, Marcel wasn't there anyway. I mean, I wasn't happy about Cerise—what had happened to her. It was horrible. But if she was gone, then maybe Marcel would . . ." Sophie let out a sigh. "But no one knew where he was. And then I became friends with Manon. With the way she looks, she needs someone to be with her—help her get stuff done. She's had it really hard." Her voice broke again.

"I bet." Claire didn't think about Manon and Richard much, how much harder their lives had been. Especially Manon. Richard could almost pass for his late teens, if you didn't look at him too closely.

"I guess that'll get easier now," Claire said.

Sophie looked at her, sniffling. "What do you mean?"

Claire shrugged. "They're aging."

For a minute Sophie just looked at her uncomprehendingly. She blinked a couple of times and then frowned. "What are you talking about?"

Now Claire was surprised. She would've thought this news would have spread like wildfire. "Richard and Manon are aging since the rite. I saw Richard last night or this morning, around three or so, coming out of Lafitte's. It took me a second to figure out what was different. But then I realized he looked older. When's the last time you saw Manon?"

"Friday, at Axelle's. She hasn't let me come over since then."

"Today's Monday—a week since the rite. When you see her, you'll notice it."

"But that's impossible! Why didn't you say this earlier?"

"I thought you knew—I thought everyone could tell. It seems to be just those two who are actually aging. But apparently Daedalus looks like crap, and Petra definitely seems weaker, according to Luc. He's worried about her."

"But I can't believe it," said Sophie, standing up and starting to pace. "It isn't possible."

Claire shrugged. "Ooh, must be magick."

144

"Richard's *aging?*"

"Either that or all the alcohol's really taking effect on him."

"Manon?"

"Yeah. She's taller, older. She looks like she's around fifteen now."

"How long will this last?" Sophie's brown eyes were wide. "When will it stop? What caused it?"

Claire made checkmarks in the air. "Don't know, don't know, don't know."

"I've got to go see Manon!" Sophie grabbed her lavender sweater and her purse. "She wouldn't be dependent; she would feel more equal. She might not even want to die. This changes everything!" She hurried to the door.

"It doesn't change the fact that you betrayed her." Claire didn't pull punches.

Sophie stopped dead at the door and looked around, stricken.

"Her age wasn't the main problem," Claire went on, more gently. "The problem was that you put yourself first. You deliberately screwed up her plan, blew off something she really wanted because it wasn't what you wanted. Her looking like slightly less dangerous jailbait doesn't change that."

Slumping against the old wooden door, Sophie rubbed a pale hand across her eyes.

"Then what now?" She sounded defeated.

Claire shook her head. "I'm a witch, not a psychic. It's anyone's guess."

Clio

"Okay, chalice of wind, got it." I held the smooth wooden cup in my hand, rubbing my thumb on the fine grain. "Circle of ashes, check." I gestured at the burned circle on the ground, where we'd done the rite a week ago.

"Yes." Daedalus leaned on his walking stick and looked around. There were only the two of us in the middle of these woods. It was barely midafternoon, but already the autumn light made deep, slanting shadows. Things felt quiet here, hushed, as if birds and animals were giving this place wide berth.

He definitely seemed weaker to me today, and so had Petra this morning. Had it happened to all of them? There was no way to tell with Luc, with his face being so messed up. What about Richard? I frowned, thinking back. I'd seen him just two days ago. Something about him had felt different. Had he been weaker? No. But something was different.

"Anytime you're ready, Clio," said Daedalus, and I snapped my attention back to him.

"Um, where's the feather of stone?" That was how the rhyme had gone, the spell. A chalice of wind, a circle of ashes, a feather of stone, and a necklace of water.

"Richard has it. It's a knife, carved of obsidian. In the shape of a feather."

I nodded. "I saw it at the rite."

"Yes. It's been in our *famille* for hundreds of years. I'm not sure how he ended up with it. It was always used in our important circles, our days of observance. That night, Petra used it to cut Cerise's baby's umbilical cord."

"And the necklace of water? I don't remember anything about that."

"The old rhyme never specified what the necklace of water was, and that night Melita didn't clarify it. I thought that it was something real, maybe something she had found or created and imbued with deep, strong magick. I remember her wearing a necklace—a string of moonstones. It disappeared when she did. Since then, I've often wondered if that was the necklace of water. You know what moonstones look like."

I nodded.

"But Petra thought it meant something different," Daedalus continued. "Perhaps tears or blood. It was foolish to try to re-create the rite without knowing for certain what that was—or without Melita, for that matter."

He sounded resigned, sad.

"You worked really hard for a long time to create that rite," I said.

"Yes. And who knows if I'll ever have another

chance?" He glanced over at me. "Perhaps with your help."

An idea came to me then, and I put it out into the world without thinking it through. How many times in my life had I done that, sending an idea, an action, a thought out into the world, like a butterfly? And like a butterfly altering the world's climate, what effect had I had on the world so far?

"Maybe," I said slowly. "Or maybe you've been going about this all wrong."

Daedalus's eyes flashed, and he looked offended in the way that only an old-fashioned, proper gentleman can look offended. "*Pardon?*" he said coldly in French.

"I mean, you've been trying to *re-create* Melita's rite because it was the most amazing, most powerful thing you could think of. But now, two hundred and forty years later, don't you think you and Jules and Petra and Ouida could write a new spell, from scratch? It wouldn't be exactly the same, and it might not have the exact same effect. But I bet you guys could do something awesome. Come at it from a different angle." I paced around the charred circle, where nothing would ever grow again. "If Melita's rite set up the form one way, that isn't the only way to do it, is it? Like, a spell to make your vegetables grow better." I applied what I knew, having helped Nan a million times. "You can achieve the same results in lots of different ways. You can strengthen the life force of your tomato plant. Or do a spell to increase its attraction to bees so more bees come and pollinate the flowers. Or do a spell to ward off bad insects. The effect is the same, but there are lots of ways to get there."

Daedalus was quiet, watching me, and I tried not to sound like an idiot. "You know the form of Melita's rite and the elements she used. Maybe there's still something missing, something you don't know about, which is why the rite didn't work, or at least didn't work the way you thought it would. But what if you and maybe some others put your strengths together and wrote a new rite, using what you know, what you've studied for two centuries?"

"I've tried," Daedalus said, his voice thoughtful.

"When? With who? The whole Treize?"

"No. It must have been back in the thirties. And with barely half of us."

"So what do you want this rite to do, exactly?" I persisted. "Melita wanted power and immortality. But you already have power. You've got immortality. You have plenty of money. You can basically do anything you want. What do you need from this rite?"

Funny how I had never thought to ask that before.

"More power."

I stared at him. "You're already incredibly strong. What would you do with more power?"

"I would be able to work beautiful, incredible, powerful magick. I would be able to achieve whatever goal I wished. I would be independent, not needing others for anything."

I digested this for a minute. "Is this like a mega-lomaniac kind of thing?"

Daedalus was startled into laughter. "Does it matter?"

I considered this carefully. "No, not to me. Unless you were to harm or control me or anyone I loved." Thais believed that he already had, that he'd killed our father. She was certain of it, but I wasn't. Visions could always lie, if someone manipulated them the right way. But if he did anything in the future . . .

"What would happen then?" He seemed amused, indulgent.

I looked up at him, met his blue eyes that now seemed faded. "Then we would become enemies." I expected him to laugh, to dismiss me with a wave of his hand.

Instead he looked at me and stroked his short gray goatee. "I see."

We waited, watching each other, as if a challenge had been thrown down.

"So, write a completely different spell myself," he said. "It's interesting. I would have the whole Treize. And I have you, my dear. Your help, your power."

Was this a test? What was I committing to? "Yes, you would."

Thais

I looked at Kevin, sitting across from me at our small table in Botanika, and thought once again about how much I cared for him, how happy I was with him. Being with him felt clean and light, and I longed for it after having worked with Carmela. I still felt tainted by what she'd done to the orchid, and the knowledge of what was ahead of me weighed heavily on my conscience.

"I'm so glad you're feeling better," I said.

"Me too. They still don't know what was wrong with me. I'm supposed to take it easy, no football or track or anything. But no school for another week! And it's only Monday. That rocks."

"I know," I said, smiling. "And your car will be okay?"

Kevin made a face. "The front end needs to be replaced. But insurance will cover it."

"Yeah—it wasn't your fault."

It was mine.

But I'd been learning limitations, how to keep magick focused so it didn't affect others. . . .

My latte was too hot. Nervously, I placed my

fingers against the tall mug and mentally crafted a limitation around it. Then I cooled it, drawing the heat into my fingers. I watched Kevin carefully—he seemed okay. *Yes!*

If I learned enough limitations, if I really studied hard or if I never worked magick around him . . .

Smiling, Kevin put his arm around my shoulders and kissed me. "I've missed you."

"I've missed you too. I was so worried about you."

"It was weird, but I'm fine now. Listen— Halloween's coming up. And the Halloween dance at school. And the haunted house at the fire station on St. Charles, by Nashville. Would you want to do any of that?"

"Oh yeah," I said. It would be so great to be a normal teenager with a boyfriend, doing "spooky" things that didn't involve actual, sometimes terrifying magick. "I just have to check with my grandmother," I added. Halloween was the most important sabbat of the year in the *bonne magie*. I was sure a big circle or celebration was planned, and I had no idea if I would be able to make the school dance. Or if I would still be with Kevin by then.

"Great. We'll need costumes. But nothing stupid, like salt and pepper. More like, I'll dress up like rice."

"Rice? What do you mean?"

He grinned. "You go as 'white,' and I'll go as rice, and you just be all over me all night."

I laughed—he looked so pleased with himself. "Very funny!"

And this was my ongoing dilemma: If I wanted, I could choose. I could turn my back on magick, be just a girl again, with a sweet, normal boyfriend; my lifespan would be normal. My life would uncomplicate itself; my future would simplify. All I had to do was choose.

Kevin stroked his fingers up my arm. "What are you thinking about?"

About how I'm lying to myself. I smiled at him. "Just enjoying being here."

"Me too."

And so it went. I was on a seesaw, teetering between safety and desire, selflessness and selfishness. Right now, selfish desire was winning. I felt good with Kevin—calm, comfortable. Everything I hadn't been with Luc. Kevin was a cozy hearth; Luc had been a wildfire.

Wildfires destroyed everything in their path.

Kevin and I were talking about going to see a movie when I suddenly felt, *Axelle.*

Turning, I saw her and Manon coming out of the book section. Axelle's eyes caught mine, and she smiled and waved in a patently artificial way. I smiled and waved back, just as artificially, and then smiled at Manon.

Good Lord. Was that Manon? It had to be—it was her, definitely, but . . . she was *older.* Not instantly recognizable as a child. She was . . . a teenager. She raised her eyebrows at me and smiled in a friendly way, and I pretended to let my jaw drop open. She grinned and nodded, and they went toward the exit.

"Do you know them?" Kevin asked.

"Remember my crazy guardian when I first got here? The dark-haired one was her."

"Oh. Yeah, not very motherly. Or parently in any way."

"Nope." Just then, I felt Axelle in my mind and almost jumped. I could literally feel her, as if she were trying to eavesdrop, to know what I was thinking. I was shocked and in the next instant wondered if she had done that when I lived with her, but I hadn't known it. Maybe the reason I could feel what she was doing now was because I'd become more sensitive to magick.

Which was amazing. But I didn't want Axelle in my head and tried to remember what I'd been taught about that. I could put up walls around myself. Clio had told me that the Treize pretty much blocked their minds all the time without thinking about it.

I quickly put up barriers around my mind—a small spell that wouldn't stop anything big or powerful but would prevent casual eavesdroppers. At once I felt Axelle's presence disappear. As she left Botanika, she cast me a thoughtful glance, as if surprised by this show of strength.

That's right, be surprised, I thought smugly.

"Uh . . ." Kevin said.

I looked over at him and realized with horror

154

that he looked gray. Oh no. I had done it again! I had done magick without protecting him, and now he was paying for it.

"Oh God, Kevin, I'm sorry!" I blurted, putting my arm around his shoulders. Instantly I dropped my magickal barrier.

He blinked several times as I rubbed his back and felt overwhelmed with guilt.

"Do you want some ice water?" I asked. He nodded and reached out with a shaky hand. After he drank some water, he took a deep breath and shook his head, already looking better.

"I'm okay," he said, but he sounded concerned and upset.

It was all my fault. I was literally damaging him, hurting him, by being around him. Kevin was the nicest guy in the whole world, and I was hurting him carelessly again and again. Seriously hurting him.

I had to break up with him.

We drove to his house in his dad's car. I said I would walk up to St. Charles and catch the streetcar home—I didn't want him driving by himself. The whole way to his house, I tried to get the nerve to go ahead and break up, but I just couldn't. He was upset and worried about his "relapse," and I felt like breaking up would be kicking him when he was down. I couldn't even think of a good reason to give him. Not one good reason.

Overwhelmed and miserable, I kissed him goodbye

and walked down the LaTours' driveway to the sidewalk, trying not to sob.

I was an idiot. A dangerous idiot. This was what Clio and Petra had been talking about, how unschooled I was, how dangerous it was to know just a little bit of magick. I was a bullet, careening around, hurting people right and left without meaning to.

I started crying, trying to hide it. Getting on a streetcar with a bunch of strangers seemed totally unappealing. Instead I kept walking uptown on Prytania Street, trying to distract myself with the incredibly beautiful houses along this section.

A car honked behind me, but I ignored it. Sometimes frat guys from Tulane or Loyola drove around honking at girls, yelling stuff. If they pushed me, I was going to rip into them.

"Thais!"

I turned to see Clio waving at me through the open window of our rental car. She immediately pulled up next to me. My first thought was, *Thank God, my sister,* and then I remembered I was still mad at her and turned away.

"Thais! Get over here!"

Sighing, I went and leaned in the open window. "What."

"What is the matter with you?" she asked. "You're walking along crying, and you won't even come over to the car? What's going on?"

I just shook my head.

"Get in the car," she said briskly, sitting back and checking her rearview mirror.

Unable to fight anymore, I got in.

Clio pulled quickly out into traffic, making people honk. She flipped a general bird out the window and took a left, heading toward Magazine Street. It was a relief to be sitting down, even a relief to be with my sister. Glancing at her, I saw she looked pale beneath the summer tan that hadn't faded much.

"What did you do today?" I asked, sniffling. *Study much?*

"This and that," she said offhandedly. "I was going home, but why don't we go to PJ's, get some coffee? I feel like I haven't seen you in ages."

I'd been avoiding her for days, since I'd heard her at Daedalus's. "Whatever." But I felt glad that maybe we could clear the air now. I sniffled again, wiping my eyes with my hand.

PJ's had a back courtyard with rickety metal tables and overgrown plants that made it feel jungle-like. I got an iced tea and we took our drinks out back.

"Okay, now tell me what's going on," Clio said once we sat down.

"I don't know where to start." With, *I'm killing my boyfriend because I'm stupid and out of control? Or, I'm studying dark magick with a creepy stranger so I can get revenge on a murderer with whom my own sister studies? Or even the old standby, I lost my dad and moved two thousand miles away and sometimes I'm still not on my feet yet?*

Pick one.

"I tried to break up with Kevin," I said. "But I

157

couldn't get the words out. I feel like I don't have any reason to give him."

Clio stirred her coffee, thinking. "How about, I met someone last summer before you, and we broke up, but I really loved him, and now he wants to get back together. So, 'bye?"

I frowned at her. "What are you talking about?" Did she mean Luc?

Clio shrugged. "It would be an excuse."

"It would be awful! It would make me look like—" I shook my head. "That's the thing. Any reason I give him is going to make me look bad. I care about him so much. I don't want him to hate me."

"You're kind of between a rock and a hard place," Clio said. "Tell him you need to take a little break because you're under so much pressure with school and your new family and stuff. Then later, when you have all your limitations and barriers down cold, you can look him up again."

She was actually trying to help me. I thought about it. "That's not bad. How long do you think it'll take me, with the limitations?"

"Well . . . like, two years?" Clio made a "sorry" face. "That's to be really good, to be able to have them up most of the time without thinking about it."

"Great." Mentioning barriers made me think of what had set all this off. "Oh my God—just now, Kevin and I were at Botanika, and we saw Axelle and Manon. And get this—Manon looks like she's about fifteen. She's older!"

Clio's eyes widened and her brows raised. "Really? It was obvious?"

"Yeah. I mean, she's taller, she's getting boobs— she's a teenager! Isn't that weird? Do you think it's happening with all of them?"

"Well, Nan *seems* older, for sure," Clio said, looking thoughtful. "Richard, I don't know about, because I haven't seen him. Who else have we seen recently? Luc, you can't tell because of his face."

What about Daedalus? How did *he* look? I wanted to say. It was hard sitting here, knowing she had this huge secret from me. But I had a huge secret too, I admitted. True, I wasn't studying with someone she hated, someone who had killed our father, but I also knew that Clio wasn't convinced Daedalus really had. It was hard to blame her for not believing my vision. Reluctantly I remembered that I hadn't really believed *her* vision. So we were kind of even in a way. I sighed, not knowing what to do with all my conflicting feelings.

"Yeah," I said, trying to remember if I'd seen anyone else. "God, if she and Richard age, it would make their lives so much easier. But . . . do you think they're aging, like, until death?"

"I don't know. All kinds of stuff happened at that stupid rite that we don't know about—everyone did something different, caused different things to happen."

"Yeah. It's all so complicated."

For a couple of minutes we sat there, lost in our own thoughts.

Clio looked up at me, her eyes green and clear. When I'd first met her, we'd seemed so identical I'd practically fainted. Now when I looked at her, I found her very familiar, but it wasn't like looking at myself. We're such different personalities that she didn't seem like another me.

"The thing is," she said slowly, "I'm not sure who to trust anymore. I always thought I could trust Nan, but she lied to me my whole life. I thought I could trust Luc. Ha. I sort of thought I could trust Richard. I thought I could trust our circles. Now I don't trust anything—except myself. And you."

"You trust me?"

"I do." She paused. "We're twins, identical twins. Two halves of one whole. I feel like I have to trust you. Listen—I think we should make a magickal pact, where we each swear to not betray the other."

"Are you serious?"

"I'm telling you—you can trust me, no matter what. Trust that I would never do anything to hurt you."

What about studying with Daedalus? I wanted to shout. But she seemed so sincere. . . . This was all making my head hurt.

"I want to know for sure that there's one person in the world *I* can trust, and that's you," she went on. "Will you swear with me? We could do a spell."

"Yeah, because we haven't gotten thrown across a room lately," I said.

She frowned. "Thais, this is important."

I thought it through carefully. Six months ago,

I'd have thought I could trust anyone in my family, anyone I was related to. I would have trusted most people. Now—it was true: there wasn't anyone I felt a hundred percent certain about. Could I really trust Clio? Could she really trust me? Nothing was that certain to me anymore . . . but I did still feel in my gut that neither of us would ever *purposely* hurt the other. I knew I could count on that.

I nodded. "Yeah, okay. We'll do a spell. And we'll swear to each other, on our mother's grave, that we'll never betray each other, no matter what. That whatever happens, we'll have each other's back. Right?"

Clio stood up, looking relieved. I was touched that this meant so much to her. "Right. Let's go do it. By the way—where *is* our mother's grave?"

"No idea."

Maman

Goddess, she was exhausted. Petra put down her bag and smoothed a hand over her silver hair. The house was empty—she'd felt that as soon as she'd come through the front gate. Perhaps Thais was with Kevin, breaking up with him. It was sad, unfortunate. Kevin was a nice kid. It wasn't Thais's fault that she hadn't grown up with the craft and didn't know how to control her power.

It was Petra's fault.

But if she hadn't split them up, they might very well be dead now. It was only chance that they hadn't been killed in the last two months, first by Richard and then by . . . whom? It was still unclear. Oddly, Petra had been unable to discern any culprit among the Treize, and it certainly seemed like the attacks had stopped.

Well, it was all twigs down the river at this point. She was doing the best she could.

In the kitchen, Petra put the kettle on. What did she feel like having? Her joints ached; she felt scattered and unfocused; she was bone-tired. . . . She laughed wryly. She could drink her whole pharmacopoeia and it wouldn't help.

She was weakening and perhaps on the downhill slide toward death. Actual death, after so long. It was a bizarre thought. What would happen to the twins if she died? Once again, Petra damned Daedalus for setting all this in motion.

Glancing at the light outside, Petra saw that she had maybe an hour before something had to be done about dinner. Where were the girls now? She wasn't exactly worried; things had been more or less quiet since the rite. But . . . everything that had once seemed solid now felt tenuous, rickety, as if it might fall apart at any moment. She'd spent centuries getting to this place, where she could create a good life. She'd brought up Clio here. After such a disastrous experience with motherhood the first time, it had taken more than two hundred years for her to want to do it again. But somehow, when she'd seen Clémence die, seen the two tiny babies take their first breaths, she'd known that these were the ones she would save. She would somehow try to break the curse of Cerise's line.

Clio had been six months old when her birthmark had appeared, on her left cheek. Cerise's birthmark. Petra's mother had had it and her grandmother. Their line was marked.

The kettle whistled, making Petra snap back to the present. She took a bag of plain Earl Grey tea and dropped it in her cup, then poured steaming water over it. The scent rose through the air on a ribbon of steam: the magick of tea.

Petra had invested almost eighteen years in Clio,

163

and now she had Thais as well. These were two children she would not see die, or turn to the dark side, or disappear.

Petra poured some tea into the plain white saucer on the table. She concentrated, closing her eyes, building the scrying spell for the girls she thought of as daughters one elegant layer at a time. Like anything else, magick was a skill. It could be done badly or done well. It was the difference between a rough-hewn, three-legged milking stool cobbled together by a farmer and the highly polished burl maple of a Boston highboy, with its perfect proportions, joints like the tail of a dove, and wood as smooth as silk.

Opening her eyes, Petra gazed down into the pale, shallow liquid. Faint tendrils of steam rose from it, and when they cleared, Petra saw Clio and Thais sitting, their heads together, talking seriously. Thais picked up a glass and drank. There were plants in the background. Clio said something, and they both laughed.

They were fine. Petra exhaled deeply, feeling tension slowly uncoil from her bones. She lifted the saucer to pour the tea back into her cup, but another image, unsought, was forming.

Petra watched in astonishment as a beautiful face, framed by waves of hair as black as her eyes, formed within the shallow saucer.

Her heart slowed to three beats per minute. Petra couldn't breathe as she absorbed the details of that face, the face she hadn't seen in 242 years.

The face smiled, showing even white teeth. "Maman," Melita said. *"Comment ça va?"*

164

Could This Be Happening?

Daedalus stopped and took his bearings. As often as he'd been in this cemetery, still, the way the sunset was dappling the tombs made things look different. A large angel had fallen off a mausoleum dedicated to firefighters, and that had made him miss a turn.

Could this really be happening now, when he was nearing his own personal sunset? Or at least felt it possible for the first time? Everything was coming together, happening all at once, and it was incredibly exciting and gratifying. Having the whole Treize, having Clio studying with him, so eager to learn . . . This was the least discontent he'd been in decades.

Ah. Daedalus stopped in front of his family tomb. Clio had teased him about his name—how he didn't use "Planchon." Everyone knew him only as Daedalus. "Like Cher," Clio had said, with an impertinent smile. No one had teased him in a very long time. It both irritated and amused him. As usual, he lowered himself onto the small cast-iron bench directly across from the nameplate. It was from a different lifetime, the lifetime when he'd had a brother and his brother had been secretly married to the strongest, darkest witch anyone had ever seen.

Now—242 years of history were coming together, right here. Daedalus had a front-row seat. In fact, he was the ringmaster.

He felt her before he heard the almost-silent footsteps on autumn-dry grass. A deep thrill went through him—this was almost unimaginable, what was happening. Every tiny hair on his arms rose. He felt so tightly strung with tension that if he stood up suddenly, his bones would snap.

There she was.

He didn't turn as she seemed to glide across the grass toward him. In the deep shadows of new sunset, he saw her place a white rose on his brother's tomb.

Finally he spoke. "I'm here, as you directed."

She turned and, if possible, was even more beautiful than he remembered. Unusually tall for a woman from their time, slim, dark-haired, and black-eyed—she favored her father much more than she did Petra, and Armand had been an incredibly handsome man.

He remained seated as she bent down to brush kisses against each cheek. When she sat next to him, he picked up the scent of spices he couldn't name.

"Of course you are." Her voice was at once foreign and frighteningly familiar, the voice that had commanded more dark magick than he'd seen before or since. "Now, tell me everything."

Thaïs

"You've come very far, very fast," Carmela said as I sat, dazed, my eyes on the black candle that only moments before I had actually levitated. By myself. I felt drained and queasy, as usual.

"I've been practicing," I said, wondering if taking Dramamine would interfere with magick. I also wondered if my eyes had changed so that I could now see in the dark. I was in the same dark red, windowless room that Carmela had first led me to. Then I'd felt like I was moving through fog, unable to see more than a foot in front of me, unable to see Carmela clearly.

Now, after working with her for only five days—was today Wednesday? Thursday? It was hard to keep track without the regular school rhythm—I felt like a cat, able to see in complete darkness. I'd worked with Carmela every day this week, sometimes for five or six hours at a time, sometimes for only an hour or two, depending on how long I could sneak away. I'd learned more in this past week with her than the last two months with Petra and Clio.

"You come from a long line of witches?" Carmela asked, picking up the black candle and setting it back in its stand.

"Yes."

"Light the candle."

I loved doing this. I'd done it for the first time yesterday, after Carmela had explained how it worked. Basically, everything exists all the time all around you, wherever you are. Every element, every substance can be called out of "nowhere" because it already exists and is there for the taking. Magick is simply a way to call something to you so that it takes on a form or substance.

I focused on the wick, already burned black. Closing my eyes, I pictured tiny molecules of the element fire all around me, infinitely small, dispersed so widely that they had no form, no cohesion. I began a spell to gather them to me, then direct them to the wick, then coalesce them into something strong enough to take form and ignite.

The best part? This took about twenty seconds. Carmela had made me do it over and over yesterday until it became second nature, like plucking a feather out of the air.

I opened my eyes in time to see a teardrop of fire swirl around the wick, lighting it. This one candle seemed to light the room like a stage because I was so used to the darkness.

Carmela's bright black eyes were on me.

"What?" I said.

She gave me an odd half smile and shook her

head, still wrapped in its African-print turban. "I enjoy our lessons, Thais." She sounded bemused.

"Oh. Does it . . . bother you, what I want to do?"

"Strip an old man of his powers? No." Carmela laughed, the sound echoing off the painted walls. "I've done far, far worse." Immediately her face was solemn, and a chill made me shiver.

Yes, of course you have, I thought, remembering that I was afraid of her.

"No. It's just—you're very strong, unusually strong in a way I haven't seen in a long time," she went on. "I enjoy it. It seems familiar. You remind me of someone I used to know."

I didn't know what to say to that. "When do you think I'll be able to do it? Strip him of his powers?"

"Sooner than I had imagined when you first asked me to teach you," she said.

"When?"

"Perhaps even . . . on Monvoile?" she said. "I can't be exact."

I nodded. Monvoile—Halloween—was about two weeks away. "That would be perfect."

"Today you're ready to practice on something more complicated than a plant," said Carmela. Standing, she went to the small black table by the door and picked up a basket that I hadn't noticed. She set it in front of me. Timidly I peeked inside, expecting a snake or something to leap out. But it was empty. I looked harder, and then in the basket's black interior, two amber eyes blinked. Instinctively I jumped; then my brain processed that they were cat eyes.

Smiling, Carmela reached into the basket and pulled out a sleepy black kitten. "Cats and humans are similar enough that if you can strip it of its power, you'll be seven-eighths of the way to being able to do it to a person."

I stared at her and at the chunky, fuzzy kitten that was now wandering within our drawn circle, unable to cross its barrier. "You want me to strip this cat of its powers?" I asked. After the orchid, I'd felt repulsed and tainted and had gone to sleep crying. Two days ago we had done an earthworm. After *that*, I'd felt almost crazy. You'd think an earthworm—slimy, faceless, not cute—wouldn't even cause a ripple across your conscience if you stripped it of its powers. I mean, it wasn't like I'd killed it.

It had still been alive when I finished.

I had thrown up outside in the alley. And again in the gutter after I'd pulled the car over. About a stupid *earthworm*. How would I feel after I took magickal power from this kitten?

"Use the same form as before," Carmela said in her rich, slightly accented voice. "When you get to where you identify your subject, I'll fill in the words to cause the spell to surround this cat." Absently she stroked the kitten's black fur, and it arched slightly and purred.

I looked up at Carmela's dark eyes. She was watching me intently. This was a test, of course. How far was I willing to go? How far into the darkness? What I wanted to do to Daedalus would take me very far down the road of dark magick. So far

170

that I might not ever be able to return. I knew that. I wanted to do it anyway.

By stripping this cat of its magick, I would be closer to my goal.

The cat was a mammal, a vertebrate. If I could do it to a cat, then I could do it to Daedalus. The cat sniffed closer to the lit candle. I felt its consciousness, its simple feline instincts. It was alert but not afraid.

I sat back. "No."

Carmela frowned. "No? No, what?"

"I'm not going to do the cat. The orchid and the earthworm were bad enough."

A look of surprise transformed Carmela's face so that it looked almost . . . clear for a second. Not so . . . well, blurry. She frowned, and her eyes narrowed. "Thaïs," she began, a dangerous, impatient note in her voice.

I raised my chin. "This cat is an innocent creature. I won't do it."

Carmela opened her mouth, but I interrupted her.

Leaning forward, practically over the candle's flame, I said, "Look, don't question whether I can do this to Daedalus. He killed my father and ripped my life in half. Believe me, when it comes time, I'll be able to strip his powers without a second's hesitation." My voice was tense, taut—I felt unlike myself. Stronger, more ruthless. "Daedalus is guilty and deserves what he gets. Every person, every human, is guilty. No animal is."

All I could see were her black eyes, which were focused narrowly on me.

"You believe every person is guilty of something?"

I thought for a moment. "Maybe not little kids," I conceded. "But even they have the capacity to be evil, to do wrong. Animals don't. The cat is out of the question."

"You believe that you'll be able to put your squeamishness aside and take the magick of another person because of how guilty you think he is?"

"Yes." I had no doubt about that. It was hard and even devastating to realize that about myself—that I was in fact willing to perform this heinous, horrific act on another person for revenge. But I was coming to terms with it.

I stood up and broke our circle, not caring if my lesson was over for today. I put on my jean jacket, then picked up the kitten and tucked it inside. I still had that hollow, sick feeling that seemed almost incessant these days, but I managed to stay on my feet without swaying. I turned to look at Carmela, barely able to see her sitting deep in the shadows of the room.

"I'll be back," I said. "Tomorrow."

I walked down the old curving steps that led from Daedalus's apartment to the courtyard below, holding on to the rail for balance on my shaky legs. I felt like crap. Again. Though it was beginning to feel less intense, as Daedalus had promised.

I'd parked the rental car three blocks away on another street and at the time had congratulated myself on my clever stealthiness. Now, of course, realizing I had to walk three blocks (even short Quarter blocks), I cursed myself. It was barely five o'clock, but clouds covered the whole sky and made it seem later. When I passed a tiny corner store, I bought an orange soda and chugged it. The jolt of sugar immediately made me feel stronger, and by the time I got to my car, the bottle was empty and I felt vaguely human.

A tall weeping willow hung over a brick wall, shading the sidewalk where I'd parked my car. I unlocked the door and practically fell into the front seat, so thankful to be sitting down. Goddess, I needed to get my act together before I drove home. This wasn't like being drunk, where I could do a spell to clear out my blood. This I just had to get through. I needed to go home and get under a hot shower. Though Nan was still weak and preoccupied, Thais had quit freezing me out since our pact. I still felt bad about studying with Daedalus, knowing how much she didn't want me to, but it was getting easier to not feel as guilty about it.

"What the hell are you doing with Daedalus?"

The tense, quiet voice from the backseat made me jump about a foot and stifle a shriek. Even before I hit the seat again, my brain had registered that it was Richard, that he had somehow gotten into my locked car, that he'd waited for me.

"What the hell are you doing in my car?" I shot back, my hand to my chest as if it would slow down my electrified heartbeat. Then I really looked at him and almost gasped again.

He *was* older, like Thais had said about Manon. Richard was *older*. I mean, of course he was ancient. But he'd always looked like a kid, about fifteen. Now he was bigger—his baggy clothes seemed almost too small. His face, once smooth and almost pretty, had harder planes. He still looked young, under twenty, but so, so different.

And he was *stunning*. I was so taken aback I just gawked at him while my brain went, *Damn, he's hot.* Then I shook my head to clear those thoughts and remembered to frown at him.

"Yeah, I know," he said. "I look older. What the hell are you doing with Daedalus? And why do I think it's something incredibly stupid and dangerous?"

174

"You do look older," I said snidely. "I can't wait to see what you look like when you're two hundred and forty-two. And what makes you think I'm doing anything with Daedalus?"

"If I keep going, I'll be two hundred and fifty-seven," he corrected me. "Maybe because I saw you go into his place six hours ago and just saw you come out. And you look like *that*." He pointed a finger at me.

Irrationally, I thought about what I usually looked like when I left Daedalus's apartment (pale and sick) and wished I looked better. I hated Richard seeing me vulnerable, not at my best. Then his words sank in.

"Are you *stalking* me now?" I put total outrage into my voice.

"Yes." Richard actually climbed over the seat and dropped down next to me. He was at least three inches taller and maybe fifteen pounds heavier than he had been—it was hard to tell.

My cheeks heated. I wanted to kick him out and race home, but if I did anything too vigorous, I was pretty sure I would hurl.

We faced each other with narrowed eyes.

"What do you want?" I said impatiently.

He looked at me so intensely that I leaned back an inch, and then his beautiful, hard mouth smiled. My breath caught. Slowly he looked me up and down, like he'd done before, and I crossed my arms over my chest when his gaze lingered.

"Stop it and get out," I said, trying to sound bored.

He leaned against the car door, calmer, not as

angry. No one had ever defied me as much as Richard did every time I saw him. It was infuriating.

"Okay, if you won't get out, I will." I wrenched open the car door and got out, then realized of course that I had nowhere to go. Richard came and stood face-to-face with me on the sidewalk.

"What are you doing with Daedalus?" he demanded.

"Nothing."

He changed tactics. "Why'd you tell ole Luc that we'd had sex?"

Oh my God—I had managed to forget about that. It all came back in a rush, what I had shouted angrily when I left their apartment. *Crap.* My face flushed with embarrassment. Good—at least I wasn't pale and pasty anymore.

"To shut him up. Now it's your turn. Go away." I looked for an escape route—and saw a small wooden door set into the brick wall I was parked beside. Someone's private garden. I leaped for the door, pushed it hard, and tried to slam it in back of me.

Effortlessly, Richard held the door open. "I don't scare off that easy," he said, pushing his way in, shutting the door behind him.

I looked for another way out, trying not to show how mad and sick I felt. This was me, *Clio*, actually on the run from someone. This had never happened before—I was a different, weaker person, and it was freaking me out.

176

A marble bench gleamed faintly in the twilight, and I sank down on it before I fell down.

"Please go away." I rubbed my eyes, keeping my hands over my face.

Slowly he pulled my hands away, waiting until I looked at him. I wasn't used to older Richard, his appearance.

"Daedalus can't be trusted." His words were quiet, and in the shadowed garden, it felt like we were the only two people alive.

I swallowed. "I know." But of course, I *was* trusting him.

"He has his own agendas that you can't know anything about." With big-cat grace Richard sat next to me, and I felt his warmth from inches away.

"What do you mean?"

"Daedalus is playing out a couple of centuries of history right here, right now, in this city. You and Thais are caught in the middle of it. I don't know what he's doing or what his plan is, but I do know that when the hellfire shows up, the only person he'll save is himself."

I didn't understand. There was so much that wasn't clear. I swallowed. Why did Richard seem so incredibly caring sometimes and so angry and bitter other times? Why should I trust him when I knew he'd tried to hurt me and Thais? I looked at him, his dark brown eyes, hair still tortoiseshell-colored, summer-streaked, his skin still tan.

"What hellfire?" I asked.

"I don't know. I just know he's got something going. And it won't be good for anyone but him. I mean, I can't help caring about the old bastard. He's helped me out of some hard places. But in the end, he would gladly throw me into the furnace if it would save his ass."

"Why are you telling me this?" The bench was hard and cold. I was exhausted and prayed that I wouldn't end up crying.

"I don't want you to get hurt."

"You mean, by anyone else but you?"

His face didn't change; he wasn't going to rise to my bait.

"Clio," he said very seriously, "I don't want you to get hurt."

"Why? Why do you care?" Impatiently I met his eyes, took in his new face again. "Why are you even *here?*"

I saw his indecision.

"Because you want to use me against Luc? Because you care about Petra and she'd be upset if something happened to me? Because you'd rather hurt me *yourself?*" I was fed up—fed up with him, with everyone, with feeling this way.

"No!" He was frowning again, taking on his look of perpetual irritation. "You know that's not true."

I stood up. I was done. I was leaving, and if he still hassled me, I would—

Typically, he moved fast, standing and yanking my car keys away. He stuffed them into his pants pocket as I gaped at him.

"What the—"

"Shut up," he said, holding me hard by the shoulders. "You know I—" He looked like this was really costing him, and I thought, *Good.* "I—want you."

My mouth almost dropped open. "That's it? That's the big drama? Give me my damn keys back! Of course you want me, you idiot! Everyone wants me! What are you—"

"I'm not *everyone*," he interrupted me furiously. "You stuck-up, full-of-yourself bi—witch! This is *me*! I don't want *anyone*. I don't *love* anyone. I don't need *anything*." He took a deep breath. "I'm telling you that—I . . . want *you*. I—" He looked awful, as if saying this was ruining his life. Wait a second, was he trying to say that he . . . ?

I didn't know what to think. Richard had loved Cerise, a long, long time ago. As far as I knew, he hadn't loved anyone since, though I was sure he'd been with a million people.

What did this mean? Was he setting me up? If he was serious, how did I feel about it?

"I know you think you still love that joker," he said, his voice bitter.

I did still love Luc. I would always love him.

"But he doesn't even see you."

"What does *that* mean?"

Richard's face was hard and set. "He looks at you and sees . . . Thais's sister."

My eyes flew wide. "Shut up, you bastard!" I spat. "You don't know anything about it! You don't know me or him or anything!" On top of the intense magick I had made today, this was pushing me over the edge. I rushed toward the exit, not caring that he still had my keys.

"Clio!" Richard's hand held the garden door shut, and he expertly dodged my kick aimed at his shin. "I'm not trying to hurt you or make you upset." His voice was oddly quiet and gentle.

"Well, you've goofed, then," I snapped, trying to kick him again.

"Why does it have to be like this?" Richard's voice was loud, exasperated. "I'm trying to talk to you! There's something between us—there always has been. Why can't you just calm down and see it?"

"Because you're a jerk?" I guessed.

"Clio." The one word was warm, inviting, and alarms went off. "We're two of a kind, you and I. You don't want Luc—he's cold. You want me. You and me—we're fire together."

Oh no, I had enough time to think, and then of course Richard was reaching for me, and of course I wasn't going anywhere, only half pretending to push away from him. He gathered me to him easily, slowly, giving me time to protest.

"No—stop," I whispered as his head came lower. Already excitement was igniting in my chest, my body recognizing him. It was *so stupid*, how I gave in so easily, but he was the only thing in my life that felt good right now.

Richard stopped and looked at me, how I was waiting for him to kiss me. "You always say that," he said softly. "You never mean it. You want me."

There was no way I could admit it.

One hand curved around my lower back, pulling

me closer to him. I felt his height, his new muscled weight—he was so familiar, but different.

"Ask me to kiss you," he whispered, his soft hair brushing against my skin.

I couldn't.

"Ask me, and I'll kiss you," he coaxed, so softly I could barely hear him. "You can have anything you ask for." He waited, and I still couldn't say anything, but inside I was trembling, aching for him. Like I always did, despite everything.

"Whatever you want," Richard said, his words setting off tendrils of anticipation along my nerves. "All you have to do is ask."

Oh goddess, I hated myself. And I wanted him so much.

"Kiss me." My words had hardly any sound, but it was enough. His mouth came down on mine, firm and warm, and his arms tightened, as if keeping me from falling off a cliff. Suddenly I felt warm and safe . . . happy and loved. It was ludicrous, some part of me knew, but I no longer cared. I wrapped my arms around him and held him hard against me. Our mouths opened and I kissed him as deeply as I could, feeling his heart speed up, his breathing quicken.

It wasn't enough. I pushed my hands under his shirt, feeling his new body with its same silken skin, same hard muscles. He groaned against my mouth, sliding his fingers through my hair, holding my head so he could kiss me however he wanted.

There, in the dark garden, I asked him for more and more, and whatever I asked for, he gave me.

One Daughter Is Alive

"You look much better." Petra sat back and surveyed her work. Next to her, Ouida nodded, her face serene. The two of them had spent the afternoon working on Luc, and Petra knew it had taken longer than usual because she'd found it almost impossible to concentrate.

She'd seen Melita, for the first time in 242 years.

Her one child, out of five, who had lived.

"Really?" Luc tried to look unconcerned, but Petra saw the hope in his eyes. She knew he was forcing himself to not jump up and look in the mirror.

She was so tired, and now her nerves were stretched to the breaking point. Ouida, as if reading her mind, got up and brought her a cup of hot black tea.

"Thank you," Petra said, taking a sip, feeling the warmth go down. She glanced at the window—it was dark out. They'd started at four in the afternoon. "What time is it?" Answering her own question, she checked the kitchen clock. Almost eight. "Where are the girls?"

On cue, Petra felt Thais on the front porch, then heard her unlock the door.

"Thais?"

Luc tensed across from her, and Ouida started clearing away their supplies.

"Hi, Petra," Thais called, sounding tired herself. She came into the kitchen. "Sorry I'm late—did you get my message?"

Petra looked at the lit-up answering machine. "No, I'm sorry—I turned the ringer off. Is everything okay?" It was more than just a casual question.

"Yeah. Hi, Ouida." Ignoring Luc, Thais reached into her jacket and pulled out a small black kitten, who blinked in the kitchen's light. "I found him in a gutter by Kevin's house," she said. "He didn't seem to belong to anyone."

"Poor thing," said Ouida. She held up the kitten and looked into its small face.

"Mew," it said.

Thais leaned against the kitchen doorway, looking wiped. "Well, I'm going to go take a shower," she said.

"Okay," said Petra. "Come down if you're hungry."

"Thanks," Thais said, turning to go.

Luc was trying not to watch Thais's every move, but clearly her presence had affected him. He stood up quickly and grabbed his jacket. "I better go," he muttered. "Thanks, Petra. Thanks, Ouida. I really appreciate it." He gestured at his face. It hadn't yet recaptured its perfection, but he definitely looked normal. People wouldn't stop and point at him at least.

Petra watched him hurry after Thais, heard him murmur something to her. She replied, but Petra couldn't hear it. She and Ouida exchanged glances. Then Thais went upstairs and Luc let himself out.

He still loved her, Petra mused. Luc, whom she'd known for so long, loved Thais. He'd always been a rake—charming, ruthless, conscienceless. She'd thought he'd given up on trying to seduce either twin, but he seemed to sincerely love Thais; Petra felt it. It made her uneasy. She needed to think about this. She had a lot to think about.

After he left, the two women sat at the kitchen table, watching Q-Tip examine the new kitten. After sniffing him cautiously, Q-Tip put one big white paw on the kitten's back, pinning him in place for a vigorous, unasked-for washing.

"Thais looked exhausted," said Ouida. "Not herself, in a way."

"Yes. She and Clio have both looked like that this past week."

"What are they doing?"

Petra was thankful for Ouida, a friend who always spoke straight. "I don't know. They won't tell me, or they lie."

"What are you going to do?"

"Wait."

Ouida nodded thoughtfully. "Are we thinking boys, drugs, sex, worse?"

"Worse." Petra had thought it over again and

again. She'd had time to come to terms with the fact that the twins were possibly getting involved in something big, magickal, and probably dark.

Thais and Clio didn't know it, but Petra had put sigils on the doorways so she could see who came and went and when. Her next step was to make a pair of gris-gris and sew them into their jackets or purses. They would help her know where they had been.

"Have you tried scrying?" Ouida asked.

Petra flinched, the memory of Melita's face coming back to her. Not that the image had been far from her mind ever since that moment she'd first seen her. She still had so many questions, so much she needed to know about where Melita had been, why she was back.

But Melita, of course, had revealed very little in that brief vision.

"Yes," Petra said aloud, remembering Ouida. "There are times when they've blocked me, when I can't see them."

"That's not good." Ouida took a sip of tea.

"No. But actually—that isn't all." Petra looked over at the woman who had been her friend for almost 250 years. She'd been holding the other information inside, trying to process her own reaction first, but she knew she had to tell Ouida before any more time passed. "Melita's back."

"Sppfftt!" Ouida sprayed the kitchen table with tea, making Petra jump. She started coughing and trying to suck in air, and Petra patted her back firmly, trying not to smile.

185

"Jesus, Mary, and Joseph!" Ouida wheezed when she could speak. "What are you talking about?"

Despite everything, Petra couldn't help laughing. Blotting up the liquid with a napkin, she said, "Melita contacted me a few days ago. She's alive—well, we were all pretty sure about that. Now she's coming to New Orleans. She wants to see me."

"Oh goddess," Ouida breathed. "How do you feel about that? I can't believe it. You must be about to climb the walls."

"Yes." Petra smiled wryly. "*Astonishment* is a small, ineffectual word to describe my feelings. I don't know." She spread her hands across her lap, trying to find the right words. "Melita is dark," she said, meeting Ouida's eyes, seeing agreement there. "I know that. I never wanted to know it back then. Never wanted to believe it. But of course I do now. I'm assuming she's very dark indeed."

Ouida looked sympathetic but didn't deny it. "What . . . did she want?"

"She wants to see me, says there's no real reason."

Ouida looked like she didn't believe that for a minute. "What are you going to do? Petra—if Melita's back and Daedalus finds out . . . If she wants to be part of the Treize for some reason—" Her brown eyes were large with worry.

"Yes," Petra agreed calmly. "Then we're fourteen, with the twins. Too many. I know. And there were the unexplained attacks on the twins, which of course I'm still considering. But I just don't believe those came from Melita. They don't seem . . . like her style, if that makes sense."

Ouida nodded slowly. "She makes lightning and earthquakes—making a planter fall on a teenager would be scut work for her."

"Yes." Petra was quiet, thinking. "She's my daughter," she said. "The only one who survived. I love her, and I'll always love her, but . . ."

"I know," Ouida said.

They're Very, Very Strong

Richard was buzzing, lit up, as he walked down the street.

Him and Clio. It was unbelievable.

Of course, he hadn't made it to 257 years old without wising up. He knew this probably didn't mean anything. Unfortunately. Or maybe fortunately. He didn't even know what he wanted it to mean. But right now, he felt great, better than great.

Looking up, he noticed he was passing Axelle's house and decided to drop in for a drink and some distraction.

Axelle buzzed him in. As he approached her front door and felt who was inside, he paused. But the door was opening, and Axelle was waving him in.

"Holy crap, look at you!" she greeted him.

"Hey." Richard suddenly felt self-conscious. He heard Manon's voice and wondered how much she'd changed since yesterday.

"Richard, ah," said Daedalus warmly. He raised a glass of sherry at Richard.

Richard smiled and eased onto a black–and-chrome bar stool, aware that everyone was examining him closely. Jules held up a bottle of whiskey, and Richard nodded. "Thanks." He took a sip, thinking that he should have just gone home, savored his feelings by himself. This had been a mistake; he didn't want to be here. One quick drink and he'd go.

Manon looked like a striking, cheerleader-type teenager. "Riche, I can pass as legal to drive. For the first time." She showed him her official license.

"Clearly there was no street test."

Manon made a face. "That was a long time ago. I'm taller; I can reach the pedals and steer at the same time now."

"That's a blessing. But good for you, Non-non."

Manon grinned at the use of her pet name. Richard wondered for a moment if Manon questioned at all how it had happened—the two of them, the only members of the Treize to begin aging. If she'd realized that the development was coming from the spell Richard had used the rite to cast, giving himself and Manon the bodies and faces of adults after all these years.

It didn't matter, really, if Manon ever knew how. He was just glad for the happiness it gave her.

And it was certainly worth it for him, seeing how Clio looked at him now. That he could finally be a man for her. With her.

"Ahem. We were just talking about the Source," Daedalus said.

Richard was so sick of the frigging Source he

wanted to break his glass. "Really? What about it?"

"I think I can open it," Daedalus said. "Not with the rite, but with a simpler spell that I'll write myself. I think it will work if it's powerful enough. But we'll need the most powerful members of the Treize."

"Like me," said Axelle, with a self-satisfied air.

"Yes," Daedalus agreed, looking like he was still getting used to the idea. "All of us here, obviously," he went on diplomatically. "And Petra's twins."

Richard's chest constricted. "Oh, come on," he said, sounding bored. "Why involve the twins? They're kids. They'll just muck everything up as usual."

"The twins are very, very strong," Daedalus said. "Together, the two of them are probably as strong as the rest of us put together. We need them. All we have to do is convince them, and that won't be hard."

"Would this be dangerous?" Jules's voice was quiet and measured.

"No." Daedalus sounded more sure than he looked.

"I'm in," said Manon.

"Why?" Richard asked. "What's the point? Isn't it kind of moot now?"

"No." Daedalus's eyes flashed. "I need the Source. I need its power to re-create the rite."

Because you're getting weaker all the time and you don't want to die, Richard thought. *Why can't you let it all rest?*

"Well, whatever," he said casually, setting down

190

his glass. "Let me know when it is, and I'll help. That is, if I'm strong enough for you." He made a sardonic face at Daedalus, and Daedalus rolled his eyes.

"Of course," the older man said.

"I'll let myself out," said Richard.

His bed had no Clio in it. Richard dropped to his single mattress on the floor, pushing aside the bunched covers. He lay on his back, one arm under his head, and started thinking things through.

When Luc came home half an hour later, Richard feigned sleep and wished he'd shut his bedroom door earlier.

"I know you're not asleep," Luc said from his doorway. He was holding a po'boy, taking bites off one end while trying to keep the drippy parts contained in its wrapper.

"Pretend I am," said Richard.

"I guess if you're asleep, you're not hungry," said Luc, shaking a paper bag.

Richard propped himself on his elbows.

"Roast beef," Luc clarified. "Dressed, tiny bit of gravy. Don't say I never gave you anything," he added dryly, heading into the kitchen.

"Damn," said Richard, getting up and following him. He sat across from Luc at their small metal table and unwrapped the wax paper. The French bread was already getting soggy with gravy. He took a big bite and savored it. "This is perfect. I wish your face had gotten messed up a century ago. It's made you so thoughtful."

"Screw you," said Luc, eating his own sandwich.

Richard thought of Clio, pulling him to her in the dark garden, kissing him, her skin hot under his hands, and very carefully didn't meet Luc's eyes.

"You missed the powwow at Axelle's," he said. "Daedalus, Jules, Axelle, Manon. They have a harebrained scheme to open the Source to boost everyone's power. And then, I guess, to redo the rite *again*. And they want to use the twins' power."

"Hmm."

Richard glanced at Luc out of the corner of his eye and saw that in fact his face really did look much better. Clearly Petra had been working her usual miracles.

"He should leave the girls alone," Richard said, watching for Luc's reaction. "They're young and don't know anything."

"Hmm."

Was Luc still pissed about what Clio had said, about sleeping with Richard? No—he hadn't even believed her. Probably. And no one knew about tonight except him and Clio.

"As annoying as the girls are, we don't want them in Daedalus's clutches," Richard pressed on.

"No," Luc agreed, chewing.

This was weird. Something was going on with Luc, and Richard didn't know what.

Which was not good.

192

On Friday, things seemed oddly normal. Nan looked better, and when she got a call to go to a case, she felt up to it. She kissed us both good-bye and warned us to be careful and to take our jackets, like we were little kids.

"What are you doing today?" Thais asked me, pouring herself a cup of coffee. She'd been asleep when I'd gotten home last night. I was glad, because I didn't want to blurt anything out—not until I knew how I felt. Did I love Richard? Were we a couple? Had it been just a onetime fluke? Did he actually care about me? Now that he'd gotten what he wanted, was he going to drop me like a hot coal?

He wasn't the only one who'd wanted it. I admitted that to myself. I'd wanted him too, so badly. Then having him, actually having sex with him, had blown my mind. I turned away so Thais wouldn't see my secret smile. My emotions were wrecked; I was confused and worried and anxious, not only about Daedalus but about everything else in my life—Nan, Thais, Luc, me. I shouldn't even have been capable of smiling at this point. But when I thought about Richard, being joined with him, kissing him, the way we felt together, how intense and incredible and even—yeah, sweet, it had been, I couldn't help smiling.

"I don't know," I answered her. "I'm feeling kind of freaked." That was honest enough. I sat down next to her at the kitchen table. "I don't know what to do with myself. Everything feels like too much, you know?"

Thais nodded soberly. "I know." She sighed heavily, and I saw the dark circles under her eyes. "I broke up with Kevin last night. On the phone."

"On the *phone*?" I mean, yeah, I had dumped guys by phone, but that was me.

She nodded, looking miserable. "I'm such a waste. But I just couldn't do it in person. I tried, a couple of times. Anyway. It was awful."

"I'm sorry. Maybe eventually you can work it out with him."

"Maybe."

The phone ringing made us both jump.

I went out into the hall and answered it.

"Clio?"

Daedalus's voice made me shiver. He'd never called me before, and I was glad Thais hadn't answered the phone.

"Yes?" I wandered into the workroom.

"Meet me at the cemetery tonight at nine o'clock," he said. "We'll do some last-minute practice before tomorrow."

"Tomorrow?" He couldn't mean . . .

"Yes, tomorrow. I've arranged for the others to meet us at the Source at six. You and I will get there first and set everything up. I'll come pick you up at four thirty."

"Four thirty?" *Please let him mean in the afternoon.*

"Before the sun comes up. We have to be ready by daybreak. Understood? I'll see you at nine."

"Yeah, okay."

That night Daedalus and I went over things I already had down cold. He was excited and even nervous, sniping at me to do everything just so. Finally we were just snapping at each other.

Daedalus rubbed his hand over his eyes. "This is pointless. Go home, get some sleep. You know it well enough."

Damn right I do, I thought.

"Fine." I gathered my tools, slipping them into the heavy silk bag I carried them in.

"Remember, be ready at four thirty," he said.

"Right."

It was a relief to leave him. I got to my car, half hoping to find Richard lurking in it again. Part of me was dying to see him and part of me never wanted to see him again.

Halfway home, I realized that what I really needed was a margarita. Yes, alcohol screwed with magick a bit, but I would have just one and then do a spell to clear it out of my system. There was no downside.

Amazingly, I found a parking spot only two

short blocks from Amadeo's. It felt like I hadn't been there in ages, and it was hopping on a Friday night. Flashing my fake ID, I got to the bar and ordered a margarita, then took out my cell phone to call Racey to come meet me.

"Fancy meeting you here."

I turned to see Claire leaning against the bar, waving a ten-dollar bill at the bartender. "Two scotch on the rocks!" She faced me and asked, "Would it be '*scotches* on the rocks'? I never know these things. How's tricks? You look like someone put you in a blender on 'whip.'"

Since I thought I'd been looking more like myself, this made me frown. I tried to see myself in the mirror over the bar, but there were too many people.

"Come on, honey," said Claire, picking up her drinks. "It's quieter in the back."

I followed her through the crowd, unable to see anything except her torn black Ramones T-shirt. In the back room I almost bumped into her when she stopped abruptly.

"Push over," she said to someone. "Make room. Look what I found."

She suddenly sat down and I saw with horror that she had been speaking to *Luc and Richard*. Both of them. Together, at this table. With Claire and now me. In a moment, I mentally zipped through the possible consequences of just turning tail and running away.

Claire smiled at me, and it almost looked like a

challenge, though not a hostile one. Richard's dark eyes were full of alert watchfulness, and I felt a flutter in my chest when I saw him. Remembering what we had done last night—how good it had been . . .

And Luc—Luc was looking better. Much better. Nan's stuff had been working. But the weird thing was . . . even though his face was closer to normal again, he just didn't seem to have that same effect on me now.

I sat down.

Claire pushed one scotch over to Richard, and he took it and drank. He seemed to be trying not to look at me, but I could feel his tension from where I sat. Luc also seemed hyper-alert, and I felt like a pinned beetle.

"Hello, Clio," said Luc.

"Hey," I said shortly, trying not to gulp down my margarita.

"No date?" Richard said, looking innocent. As usual, being the one comfortable with throwing gasoline on a fire.

I gave him a look that had once made Nan ground me for two weeks. He put on a cheerful smile, so obnoxious and audacious that I had to bite back a laugh.

"So!" said Claire, rubbing her hands together. "This is cozy! Anyone got any hot gossip?"

Let's see, where to begin. . . . I was working gray magick with Daedalus. Thais broke up with Kevin. And oh, yeah, Richard and I did the wild thing last night.

Yep, that pretty much covered it.

"I'll start," said Claire, since no one had spoken. "*A guy* asked Manon out on a *date*."

"You're kidding!" I said. "What'd she say?"

Claire's eyes widened. "I believe she said yes."

Richard groaned and covered his eyes with one hand. "Does Sophie know?"

"Not yet. But I'd give big money to be there when she finds out," said Claire.

"Claire," said Luc.

"Come on," said Claire. "This is serious stuff." Frowning slightly, she blinked and then looked at me. Moments later, Luc's eyebrows rose, and he also looked at me. I checked Richard: his eyes were locked on me.

"What?" I asked. "Did I spill something?" I checked my tight cotton sweater.

Glances passed between the three of them like lightning.

"Magick's coming off you in waves," Luc said quietly. "I just realized it was you. What have you been doing?"

Was Richard going to rat me out here?

"Just practicing," I said offhandedly. "Got my ROA coming up."

"Petra says you aren't doing it," Luc said.

Damn.

He and I looked at each other for several seconds, and without realizing it, I compared his deep blue eyes, so beautiful and expressive, with dark brown ones that made me catch on fire.

"*This* is interesting," Claire almost purred, looking from me to Luc and back again.

I felt Richard's tension coiling tighter and wondered if they could feel it too.

"Good for you, Luc," Richard said. "Save her from herself." He sounded snide and on the wrong side of angry.

Luc turned to Richard and his face hardened. "Maybe I should save her from *you*."

Richard scoffed. "Screw you." He knocked back the rest of his drink in one big gulp, and his jealousy seemed so clear and obvious that I was sure the whole bar could see it.

"No, Richard," said Luc coldly. "You're quite the lady-killer. In more ways than one."

Richard's face tightened and flushed. "You better stop now."

"Have you told her yet?" Luc pressed him.

"Told who what?" Claire asked, leaning forward.

Luc turned to me. "You said you were doing Richard." Claire practically gasped.

"Oh, please," I said, mortified.

"Luc, you don't want to go there." Richard's voice was like stone.

"Has Richard told you why that wouldn't be a good idea?"

"You mean, besides all the obvious ones?" I said, trying to save myself with sarcasm.

"Luc—" Richard said warningly.

"You're the thirteenth generation of Cerise's line," Luc went on.

Richard stood up fast, knocking over his chair. "Luc, I swear to God, if you—"

Luc's body tensed as if he knew battle was coming.

"So?" This was all over my head so far.

"Richard's family," Luc said quickly as Richard lunged. Luc leaped out of the way but kept talking. People around us turned to stare. "Richard was Cerise's baby's father. He sired your line. You're *related* to him."

My mouth dropped open. I was horribly aware of strangers watching us with interest. In the next second, Richard crashed over the table, furious, his hands going for Luc's neck. Glasses and drinks went everywhere—my margarita spilled into my lap, making me jump up. Richard managed to snag Luc's shirt, popping a couple of buttons off. One hit me on the cheek, hard. Richard had Luc on his back on our table. I could hardly take it all in.

Richard had fathered the baby Thais and I had seen in our visions, Cerise's baby. The one she had died giving birth to. That baby had been my great-times-god-knows-what-grandmother. Richard was *related* to me, like a super-great-grandfather or something. And last night he and I had . . .

Oh God. Oh, oh, oh God.

Claire jumped up too. "Boys, boys," she said, but they continued to struggle. Muttering under her breath, she stroked her fingers down Richard's arm and onto Luc. Instantly they both sagged, as if their breath had been knocked out of them. They moved in slow motion, turning to glare at Claire, whose lips were still moving, her eyes focused on them. Richard,

I was sure, was trying to curse her out but couldn't form words.

I stared at them in disbelief. Richard had *known* he was my ancestor and still had come after me. He'd known I'd probably be grossed out, but he hadn't told me. We'd actually *had sex* last night, and he hadn't *told* me.

"You bastard," I said with quiet fury, my words cutting through the noise and commotion. I leaned closer to make sure Richard heard me. "How many times are you—going to do me wrong?" That was all I could come up with—I was freaking out and close to tears.

His eyes took on a look of ravaged pain. "No, no," he said, his words slow and slurred.

"Oops! These boys have had too much to drink," Claire said brightly to our audience. She clapped as if to dispel the onlookers. "Guess I better get them home!" She grabbed Richard's T-shirt in her fist and hauled him off Luc. He came with her like a rag doll. I was already turning and pushing my way through the crowd.

I raced out of Amadeo's, suddenly feeling like the magick and the drink and being horrified was all making me ill. Somehow I made it back to my car, mumbling the words to de-alcoholify myself. By the time I cranked the key in the ignition, I was more desperate to get home than I'd ever been. I backed up to get out of the tight space, and suddenly the right-side passenger door opened and Luc threw himself in.

Because I wasn't going to learn to *lock my freaking doors* in a million *years*.

"Get the hell out of my car!" I snapped, backing up again and easing forward. I was shoehorned into a space only inches bigger than the rental car, and there was no way to peel out and leave Luc in a satisfying cloud of exhaust.

"Clio, please listen to me." He sounded pretty normal, as if Claire's spell had already worn off.

"Shut up and get out of my car!" I shouted, backing up too quickly and tapping the car behind me. Its alarm started going off, and I swore loudly.

Lurching forward, I cleared the car in front of me by a hair and finally pulled out into Quarter traffic, which was dense but pretty slow. Someone honked angrily, and someone else swerved. I headed toward Rampart Street to go back uptown, wondering how I could kick Luc out of my car like they did in movies. A satisfying image of Luc rolling in the street, all scraped up, came to mind.

"I know you're upset," Luc said, using a "calm the hysterical woman" voice.

"You think?" I snarled, taking a turn too fast, making my tires squeal.

"Slow down before you kill yourself!"

"I guess it wouldn't kill you, though, would it?" But I slowed down. Nan would be devastated if anything happened to me. I was the closest thing to a daughter she had.

I screeched to a halt at a red light and took the opportunity to reach across and pound Luc with my fist. "I don't know which one of you is the biggest jerk! I hate both of you!"

Luc winced when I hit him, then gestured at the light. "Green."

I slammed the gas pedal down and roared forward as fast as the little chipmunk engine would let me.

"Clio, listen," Luc began, sounding so reasonable I wanted to scream.

"I'm done listening to you, you jackass!" Ignoring him, I wheeled around Lee Circle and raced up St. Charles Avenue. Luc's eyes were on me, but I stared straight ahead. After several minutes I tried to calm down enough to drive less like a maniac.

"Are you sleeping with Richard?" Luc's voice was quiet inside the car.

"None of your damn business." My knuckles were white on the steering wheel.

He'd been expecting me to vehemently deny it and was shocked when I didn't.

Tough.

Finally I turned down Broadway, heading toward the river. I had no idea how Luc would get home, and I didn't care. After turning onto our street, I went two more blocks, then slammed to a halt at the curb. I leaped out of the car and slammed the door behind me.

As I rushed toward Nan's house, the streetlight overhead winked out, casting almost the whole block in darkness. In the split second I paused to look at it, Luc caught up with me. I whirled to face him, knowing that if he grabbed my arms like Richard always did, I would deck him.

"Go away," I hissed.

He put up his hands to show he wasn't dangerous. "Clio—please—just stop. I'm worried about you. I don't want Richard to hurt you or lead you on. You don't know him like I do—he might look like a kid, but he's one of the coldest, most ruthless guys I know. He makes *me* look like an innocent babe. I promise, I just want to be your friend now after all the hurt I caused."

Luc seemed incredibly sincere—just like he had all the times he'd lied to me.

I turned and walked away. I had to get up at four fifteen. After tomorrow and doing the spell with Daedalus, I would be able to rest for a while. I wouldn't have to work hard magick and feel sick afterward. I wouldn't have to lie to Nan and neglect Thais and Racey and everyone else. Life could be a teeny bit more normal after tomorrow. And I wouldn't worry anymore about Richard, about Luc, about these people I loved but could never trust.

"Clio," he called after me, but I shut out his voice as if he were a siren, calling me to smash my boat on the rocks.

Thais

It was still dark outside. Half awake, I couldn't see the moon out my window, which meant it was after 3 a.m. Then I realized that it was amazing that I even knew that and marveled sleepily to myself.

So after three but before dawn. I snuggled down into my pillow, already slipping back into my dream. I didn't know why I'd woken up. I was so tired, and this was so delicious, this almost-asleep feeling. It felt incredibly good, and—

Clio was awake.

We hadn't shared a dream, had we? I wondered, barely conscious. I lay still, my eyes closed, vaguely wondering what had woken her. My body felt like lead, my arms and legs boneless and weighted down. My bed felt perfect—the sheets were perfect, I was the perfect temperature, and I didn't have school tomorrow.

After I dozed a minute, some niggling feeling at the edge of my consciousness told me again that Clio was awake. For no reason, I forced my eyes open and focused. She wasn't sick, was she? Didn't sound like it. And everything in me was dragging me back down to sleep, as if—

As if I'd been spelled, actually.

This thought made me open my eyes again, and I ran a systems check, wondering if I would recognize a sleep spell. I thought I could—this felt like I was being cradled in a golden web of sleep, and it was drawing me down into perfect, unworried slumber.

But Clio was wide awake. Why was she awake if I'd been spelled? Had I even been spelled? Thoughts flitted out of my mind like tissue in a wind, sliding away before I could even focus on them. All I wanted to do was drift off again.

Deliberately I lay still, keeping my breathing deep and even but trying hard not to slip into unconsciousness, no matter how inviting it was. I closed my eyes and concentrated. It came to me that Clio felt nervous or excited or scared. What should I do? Could I even get up? I was afraid to try: if I were bound to my bed magickally, I would freak out and panic.

Almost silently, Clio left her room and crossed the small landing at the top of the stairs. She passed by my half-open door and padded downstairs barefoot. Something told me that everything was fine, everything was all right, that I should just go back to sleep and not worry about it.

Which made me freak out even more—those feelings were the classic signs of sleep spells, as Petra had described them to me. I fought against exhaustion, blinking again and again, and propped myself up on my elbows, even though being in a coma sounded good right now. Casting my senses, I felt that Petra, downstairs, was asleep herself.

Which meant that Clio had done this: she'd spelled the house so we would all sleep deeply. But why?

I need to wake up.

My sister had spelled me to sleep through something. I forced myself to sit up, even though my arms and legs felt like they weighed hundreds of pounds. Again came that reassuring thought: *Everything's fine, it's nothing, go back to sleep.*

Clio left the house. I felt her leave, and then I heard the faintest of clicks as the front door closed behind her. I finally thought to look at my clock. It was four twenty-five.

What in the world was she doing?

I got clumsily to my feet, feeling dopey and wiped out. I tried to think of a spell to counteract the sleep spell—I was sure there was one; I just couldn't think of it. Instead I groped my way to the bathroom and hunched over the sink, splashing cold water onto my face.

That woke me up enough to remember to draw some runes in the air—*deige* for dawn, awakening, clarity. *Uche* for strength. *Seige* for life and energy. Then I muttered:

> *Repel the fog that clouds my brain*
> *Bring me to myself again*
> *Whatever spell thus binds me so*
> *I now compel to let me go.*

Within moments I felt myself waking up. I splashed more water on my face, then remembered that Clio had already *left*. I raced into my room and pulled on yesterday's jeans and a sweatshirt, then sped downstairs as quietly as I could. I ran into the front room and looked out the window by the front door, knowing that Clio must have left minutes ago, when I was trying to clear my head in the bathroom, and that I had no hope of knowing where she had gone.

But to my amazement, she was standing in the front yard by herself. She was dressed in dark clothes, and of course her hair was dark, but I had eyes like a cat and could see her outline against Petra's plants by the fence. What the heck was she doing?

In the next instant, I raced back upstairs, taking the steps three at a time. Behind a poster in my room was a niche I'd made in the wall. My supplies were in there—my usual magick tools, plus the things I used with Carmela. I threw them into a canvas bag and rushed downstairs.

At the front window, I was just in time to see a dark blue car pull up in front of our house. Clio went out to meet it. I stared, even as I shoved my bare feet into my sneakers by the front door. When Clio opened the passenger-side door, the interior light went on.

It was Daedalus. What a big surprise. They'd been working together; now they were going to do something, put some plan in action. *Oh, Clio,* I thought in anguish. *How could you?*

I accepted the fact that I would follow them even before I consciously decided to. I grabbed the keys to the rental and hovered by the front door. As soon as they were down the block, I slipped out the front door and hurried to our car. The streets were virtually empty: they would be easy to follow, but I'd have to stay far back, since I would be obvious.

Clio, he killed our father. What are you doing?

She Will Be Pleased

Beside him in the front seat, Clio looked tired but alert. For the last forty minutes, she'd been uncharacteristically quiet, none of her usual bravado on display. He felt the tension coming off her and felt also how she was working to control it.

He was proud of her. He congratulated himself on finding her, discovering her talent, taking her under his wing. Melita would be very pleased.

"And this will open the Source?" Clio's voice was quiet but startling in the dark car.

Daedalus shot her a glance. "Yes."

"And we'll increase our power with those spells?"

"Yes. We'll take power from the nature around us, as we've practiced. Then we'll be able to take greater power from the Source itself."

Clio nodded, not looking at him.

On the farthest horizon, the sky was lightening almost imperceptibly. It would be dawn in half an hour. He would be ready. And so would Melita.

I'm not a morning person.
There's a reason I started drinking coffee when I was
five—I needed that jolt of joe to gear me up for
kindergarten. Right now I felt like my eyeballs had
been fused open. I was hyper-alert, every nerve ending
tingling, but I also felt a bone-deep weariness from a
combination of having worked hard magick again and
again and having gotten barely any sleep last night.

Each road Daedalus turned down was narrower
than the last, and by the time it was almost dawn,
we were bumping down what felt like a dirt cattle
path. I recognized where we were; he'd told me we
were going back to the circle of ashes.

"What about everyone else?" I asked as Daedalus
rocked to a halt beneath a huge live oak. I looked
around—no other cars were visible.

"They're joining us at daybreak," Daedalus said,
getting out of the car. As usual, he was dressed in
dark, somewhat old-fashioned-looking clothes and
had his walking cane hung over one arm. "We'll start
with the purity of just us two and then add others as
needed."

I looked at him and once again mentally kicked myself for having put myself into what had the potential to be an incredibly stupid, if not deadly, situation. I seemed to have a death wish of some kind, or maybe I was just dumb as an effing rock.

Daedalus popped the trunk, then leaned around to call me. "Come, my dear. It isn't far now."

This whole area felt deeply familiar, now that I'd been here less than two weeks ago—and then there were all the visions of the place that Thais and I'd had.

Well, here goes.

We cast our circle within the circle of ashes just before dawn lit the clouds with scalloped edges of pink and orange. It was almost cool right now, but it would be warm again later. Around us, some trees had lost their leaves, but mostly there were pines and live oaks. Though the woods looked scraggly, they weren't bare.

No measly candles for us—instead Daedalus kindled a small fire on the patch of bare earth in the center of the circle. We stood facing each other but not touching. Closing my eyes, I sang the spell to reveal my power, perfect and whole and strong, the inner essence of who I was. Then I felt Daedalus's power, and together we sang the bridge that twined our powers together. We weren't an even match—when Thais and I did this, it felt smooth and almost indistinguishable. But Daedalus and I were two very different beings, and I was glad we wouldn't have to do this much.

Just yesterday he had taught me the next section,

where I joined my power to the nature around me. Here, surrounded by huge trees and leaves and rocks, I would feel like the Incredible Hulk when it was over. I'd memorized the spell phonetically and recognized only about half the words. It felt very ancient, and as I sang, I realized for the first time that a dark thread ran through it. I hadn't noticed it yesterday, hadn't felt it. But now that I was here, setting it loose, its dark undercurrent set off an alarm in my head.

But the alarm vanished in the next moment as a rush of power, beautiful and pure and intense, swept me from head to foot, making me sway and gasp. Light and strength filled my chest and spread throughout my body, as if I'd been empty before and was being filled with life and oxygen for the first time. I was awestruck—this was a hundred times more powerful and intense than anything I'd done before. I felt unbearably ecstatic and at the same time overwhelmed.

I opened my eyes. Opposite me, Daedalus looked flushed, healthy, younger. He smiled faintly, eyes glittering, the rising dawn painting a golden outline around his head.

I smiled, every breath I took feeling like pure sunlight. If I raised my arms, I would float right off the ground. If I touched a flower bud, it would bloom. If I brushed my hand over the ground, sleeping insects would waken, seeds would burst with life, new plants would push through the surface. I felt like I would live forever.

I laughed, and Daedalus smiled at me, his face lit by the fire.

"It's so beautiful," I whispered. My voice was otherworldly, musical, so perfectly in tune with nature that it was barely human.

"Yes," he agreed softly. "Power is beautiful."

Colorful leaves fluttered to the ground behind him—I saw them despite the weakness of the daybreak's light. Joy rose up in me at the very idea of autumn, of seasons changing, of the endless cycle of death, rebirth, and growth. All around me, life pulsed in time with my heartbeat; I was connected to everything, one with everything, surging with power, bursting with magick.

"Now, let's open the Source." Daedalus's words came to me as a thought, a feeling, and I felt a new rush of exhilaration at the idea of creating more magick in this exalted state.

"Yes," I breathed, and the leaves falling from the trees looked like nature's jewelry. I wanted to hold out my hands and have a leaf land on me as lightly as a dragonfly.

Daedalus started his spell, first casting the limitations. The song went on for a while, and our surroundings grew more lit with each passing minute. I was paying attention to Daedalus, but the gentle sound of leaves falling distracted me, and, enchanted, I focused on one wavering in the air.

And in the next moment, I was chilled with a horror so complete it was like someone had thrown a bucket of icy water on me.

My mouth opened in an O. Quickly I looked around—here, there, all around—and had my horror confirmed. It wasn't *leaves* falling to the ground—it was *birds*. Everywhere around us, one by one, small songbirds were falling from their perches, from their nests, and dropping to the ground. Appalled, I realized that the magick pulsing with each heartbeat was in fact the power, the lives that these birds were losing to me. Each new pearl of light that swelled inside me meant that another bird had just died and that I had absorbed its power.

"Daedalus!" I choked. "Daedalus! Something's wrong!"

It took almost twenty seconds for my words to register. Slowly he opened his eyes, stilling the spell. He looked angry.

"Clio! You realize I'll have to begin again."

"Look! Look!" I pointed all around us. "The birds— birds are dying everywhere! Something's wrong! Stop the spell! Break it! We did something wrong!"

Daedalus didn't even flick a glance over my shoulder. In that second I realized he wasn't shocked, wasn't horrified. Wasn't even surprised, in fact. This was the spell he'd had me memorize yesterday: a spell to take power from birds by taking their lives and adding them to ours.

"Oh goddess!" I cried.

"Clio, don't overreact," Daedalus said more calmly. "This is what we talked about; this is what you wanted. Everything has a price, and you said you were willing to pay that price."

"Not *this* price!" Littering the ground like crumpled tissues were ten, twenty, thirty, *more* songbirds, too many to count. I knew their names, I had memorized these and so many more, as part of my working magickal knowledge. Carolina wrens, brown-headed nuthatches, thrushes, sparrows of various kinds, and even some tiny, delicate, jewel-like painted buntings, which are so rare to see. All dead everywhere I looked, and others still falling.

Tears flooded my eyes. Choking on sobs, I got out the words that would break any spell I was working. Daedalus lunged across the fire and grabbed my shoulders, looking furious.

"Stop it!" he shouted. "How dare you! Now you've made their deaths in vain! We need their power to open the Source! This is what you wanted! You don't understand! Stupid girl!" He shook me so hard my teeth rattled, but I still managed to draw the end sigils in the air, managed to get out the last words, and then it was over. Beauty, life, and power left me, and I dropped to the ground like a sack of dirt.

"You don't understand!" Daedalus cried again, sounding close to tears of rage and frustration. "You don't understand!" He sank to his knees by the fire, then dropped to all fours, gasping and trying not to cry.

"No," I said. I lay on the ground, feeling like I would never be able to move. Without magick, the whole world was in shades of washed-out gray. I was diminished to a point where I wasn't sure I was

216

human, or alive, or anything. But something had occurred to me, the answer to a puzzle. "You're the one who doesn't understand. Now I know why Cerise died that night."

"What?" he rasped, raising his head with effort. "What are you talking about? She died in childbirth! Many women did back then."

"No." I managed to shake my head, though it felt leaden. "You didn't see it—you didn't want to see it. Cerise died because Melita took her life to get her power—the power of Cerise's life is what's kept all of you alive all these years. You stupid *idiot*."

Daedalus gaped at me, his eyes now bloodshot, his face deathly pale.

"No—you're wrong," he insisted. "You don't know anything about it."

"I'm right," I said with certainty, feeling like death. "Cerise died to give you immortality. Like these poor birds died to give us power." I started to cry hard, sobs racking my chest, threatening to break my throat.

Out of the corner of my eye I saw Daedalus freeze and then look up. I focused on him in time to see confusion cross his face.

"Wha—" he said faintly.

With huge effort, I turned my head. And saw Thais, my sister, walking toward us with a wand in her hand.

Thais

The first time a dead sparrow pelted my shoulder, I gasped and jumped. The second time a little bird bounced off my shoulder, I caught it in my hands.

It was a small brown bird, nondescript, the kind you see thousands of over the course of your life. Nothing special. Its eyes were closed, feet curled, feathers soft and light and warm—a thing of beauty. In my hands it felt as grotesque and repulsive as the earthworm had after I'd stripped its powers. I smothered a shriek and dropped it, and then I saw that more were falling like rain, like slow, feathery raindrops splashing onto the wet leaves on the ground.

What was happening here?

I rushed forward, no longer trying to be stealthy. I'd followed Daedalus's car pretty easily, then parked out of sight and taken a roundabout way to the circle of ashes.

This was it. Clio would never forgive me, but this was the perfect opportunity. Carmela didn't think I was ready, but I was. I'd learned the basic form—and I'd crafted a short section that I would insert into the spell where the earthworm part had been.

Death was everywhere, morning light showing the stark corpses. I lost count of how many birds dropped around me, and I tried not to step on them. It was a nightmare, so desolate and horrible that I thought these woods would feel tainted forever.

Especially after what I was about to do.

At the edge of the woods I stopped. I heard Clio crying, saying something about the birds, and I saw Daedalus grab her and shake her hard. Trying to tamp down my anger, I quickly began the spell. It was long and took minutes to set in place, with the limitations and having to exclude Clio. I sang very softly, even after Clio dropped to the ground sobbing and I wanted to run to her. Then Daedalus fell to his hands and knees. Clio's words about Cerise came dimly to my mind, but I couldn't process them: I was ready. I aimed my wand at Daedalus and held out my left hand, which had a black silk cord wrapped around it.

I walked out of the woods toward him, and he felt it, looking up in surprise. With four words I hit him with the binding spell and pulled the cord tighter around my fingers. He froze, and part of me couldn't believe it was working.

Steadily I kept on, weaving the spell line by line, phrase by phrase. I drew runes in the air for victory in battle and the one that meant frozen, obstacle, delay. I drew sigils in the air, big, with my whole corded hand, the one that tied the spell to this place right now, the one that solidified my strength right here.

"Thais?" Clio asked brokenly, trying to get up. "What are you doing?"

I couldn't answer, but now Daedalus was wide-eyed: he knew. I felt him trying to move, to break free like a bug from a spider's web, but I held him there.

The spell was grueling, draining my energy. It was down-to-the-bone terrifying—I knew it was wrong, so wrong. There was a road in front of me: to one side was light, to the other was dark, and I was taking the dark path.

I thought about Daedalus chanting the spell that had made the car jump up onto the sidewalk. I thought about how scared my dad must have been to see it crashing toward him. It must have taken Daddy minutes to die, minutes where he thought about me, about my mom, about my twin who he thought was dead.

I hadn't been with him. He'd been gone by the time they got to the hospital and called me. I didn't have a chance to say good-bye.

Daedalus's mouth opened and his lips formed a terrified "No!" but no sound came out. Still I kept going, thinking of my dad dying, thinking of the life I'd lost. Daedalus's magick began to leave him. I caught it with my spell and began to pull. He screamed and collapsed on the ground, curling up in agony.

Clio shouted, "No, no!" and tried to get up. I

held out one hand, trapping her on her hands and knees. I'd had this all planned out for days, waiting for the right opportunity, and I had to execute it. Daedalus writhed on the ground, a tortured old man, and still I kept going, pulling his magick from him as if I were uncoiling wool from a skein. He lay among the ashes of the circle, their dust streaking his face, his hands. Clio watched the scene with astonished horror, but she was helpless to stop me.

Still I pulled it from him, and it was infinitely harder than it had been with the orchid or the earthworm. Sweat broke out on my forehead. I gritted my teeth, feeling an indescribable pain at working magick too advanced. Daedalus's power felt ancient and dark and unknown, and I knew it was so much more than what an ordinary witch would have. It flowed through my wand and I dissipated it out into the world because I didn't know what else to do with it. My studies hadn't gotten that far.

I don't know how long it took—once I started, there was no telling how much time had passed. But finally I felt Daedalus's magick lessen, his thread become thinner and weaker, and I saw his body lying like a shriveled husk on the ground. The last of it came away from him gently, dandelion fuzz releasing itself from him as lightly as air.

I had done it. I had taken my revenge on the man who had killed my father.

The spell collapsed on itself ungracefully, leaving me standing there as if I'd been hit by lightning. I met Clio's horrified eyes, saw her blur, and then I too fell to my knees onto the damp, leafy ground. The world was spinning crazily, and I dry-heaved, my stomach empty. I felt horribly ill. But I didn't care what happened now.

"Very good, child," I heard a voice say. Amazed, I looked up to see Carmela stepping out of the woods, her own wand raised.

"Who—?" Clio muttered, just as I said, "Carmela!"

"I thought you weren't ready, but you decided different, I guess," she said in her seductive voice. "It takes a lot to surprise me, but you've done it. Unfortunately, I really didn't want you to strip Daedalus of his powers—at least, not yet. I needed him. But I suppose I can improvise."

"What are you doing here?" My voice was thin and broken, and speaking made my head feel like it was going to explode. Carmela smiled pleasantly in a chilling way that awoke fear I hadn't thought I could still feel. Now that I saw her in weak daylight, her features were clear in a way they hadn't been before in the darkness.

"Melita." The word was barely sounded. I whipped my gaze to Daedalus, who was staring at Carmela with hope and, I thought, humiliation.

"Melita? That's not Melita," I said, trying to swallow. "Her name is Carmela."

Carmela smiled at me, and an icy hand seemed to seize my throat. I coughed as she shook her head fondly. "Thais, Thais," she said affectionately. "So smart, so strong, so unexpected. But not smart or strong *enough.*" She raised her wand again, pointing it right at me. "You've thrown quite a wrench in my plans."

"What plans?" I tried to say, but could barely make a sound.

She started speaking, and I felt rooted to the spot, on my knees on the wet leaves in this cursed place. Her eyes narrowed, she lifted her wand. I had time to think, *Oh God.*

"Wait!"

The voice came from the woods. Carmela and I both turned, dumbfounded. Petra rushed forward and threw herself in front of me just as Carmela snapped her wrist down. Petra's own wand was pointed at Carmela, and she was hissing words I didn't recognize.

Petra's body jolted and Carmela snapped her wrist up, looking astonished.

"Maman!" she said, which made no sense to me.

"Carmela?" I said, feeling brain-fogged.

"Carmelita," Petra said weakly, in front of me.

Darkness Reigns

Melita lowered her wand, then shook her head. Her face tight with irritation, she went and knelt in front of Petra, touching her shoulder. "Maman, tu est bête comme un chou."

Petra couldn't argue with her.

Then Melita looked over at Daedalus, who was still curled on the ground, and at Thais, who was trying to get up, her face white, eyes huge with shock.

"Carmela is Melita?" Thais managed to say, and Petra wondered with dread how on earth Thais knew her and why by that name.

Slowly Petra got up, and her daughter Carmelita helped her. She hugged Petra briefly, and Petra closed her eyes, feeling deeply how long it had been since their last hug and how she might not ever feel it again. Then, stepping back, Melita pulled off her turban. Long hair as black as Armand's spilled past her shoulders.

Again Petra looked at Thais. She was staring at Melita in shock and . . . what else? Shame. *Oh, Thais,* Petra thought. *What have you done?*

"Thais—Clio," she said. "Are you all right?"

Clio nodded, getting up with effort.

Thais struggled to her feet, swaying slightly, looking green.

"Quite the pair you have here, Maman," Melita told Petra. "They're very smart, very talented. And, of course, very, very powerful. I felt their power all the way in Europe."

"Is that where you've been?" Petra asked.

Melita laughed, and Petra saw Thais shudder at the sound. "I've been all over, Maman. Everywhere." She looked pityingly at Daedalus, who seemed to be barely breathing, then focused on Thais. "I wish you had not been so smart, so talented, and so powerful." She switched her gaze to Clio. "And you—you saw in a moment what the rest of them haven't seen in two hundred and forty-two years."

"What?" Petra couldn't help asking.

"The truth," Melita said simply. "The fact is, we're not immortal, we Treize. Your lives have only been extended for thirteen generations. Our time is running out. It's time to renew our contract for another thirteen generations." She smiled again. "That's where your twins come in, Maman."

"What do you mean, extended?" Petra asked. "I don't understand."

"Melita killed Cerise that night," Clio said, more solemn than Petra had ever seen her. "As part of the rite. She took the power of Cerise's life and gave it to all of you who were there. Now it sounds like she needs to do it again."

Petra's mouth dropped open, and she stared at Melita in shock. "No."

Melita made a regretful face. "I loved Cerise, you know I did, Maman. But I chose her carefully—*she* would die, but her line wouldn't. See? I let you have her baby, at least."

Petra couldn't speak.

"Not . . . immortal?" Daedalus's voice was so faint Petra could barely hear it.

"No," said Melita. "Just extended, for thirteen generations." She pointed at Thais and Clio. "They're the thirteenth generation. I'm here to do it again, to give us another thirteen generations of life. But I need the Treize, the twins, and . . . the chalice of wind, the circle of ashes, and the feather of stone."

And the fourth thing, Petra thought with dread.

"Unfortunately, Daedalus is of no use to me now." Melita shook her head at Thais. "I should have been more wary about someone whose darkness rivals even mine."

Petra heard Thais gasp and saw Clio look at her twin in shock.

"Don't look so surprised, Clio," Melita said. "I'm very proud of you too."

"*What?*" Petra said.

Thais hung her head, and Petra was dumbfounded. This was impossible.

"What are you talking about?" Clio asked in a choked voice.

"Of course, dear Cerise wasn't," Melita went on. "We all saw that. *I'm* clearly dark, but they're not my descendents. No, they got their darkness from Cerise's baby's father."

"Richard," said Clio. Petra had no idea how Clio knew that. Thais was surprised, though, judging by her face.

"Not Richard," said Melita.

"Marcel?" Petra felt like she needed to sit down soon before she fell.

"Not Marcel."

"But there were only those two," said Petra. "I didn't even know about Richard until recently."

"There was a third. Just once," said Melita. "Our little Cerise, all fey and light, *un papillon*. But she got around, apparently. And no one knew. Except me."

Daedalus made a choking sound.

"Yes," said Melita, her eyes gleaming. "It was none other than our village elder. Just the one time—he lost his head, she didn't resist, and now here we all are."

This didn't make sense. Petra didn't understand. "Daedalus was the father of Cerise's baby?"

"Yes," Melita said. "And anyone looking at him can tell that he's quite, quite dark. And his darkness has been passed down in that line, from generation to generation. Right into our twins."

"They're not dark," Petra said more strongly.

"Of course they are, Maman," said Melita. "Look around you. A forest full of dead birds, Daedalus stripped of his powers, your never knowing what they're doing or who they're with . . . Don't blame yourself. It's in their blood."

"They're not dark," Petra insisted, but she saw the look of guilt and shame on Thais's face. How could it be possible that she had stripped Daedalus of his powers? Oh. Because she had been studying with *Carmela*, and Petra hadn't known. Goddess, how she had failed.

"Not as dark as they're going to be," Melita said. Fast, before Petra understood what she was doing, Melita hissed a spell and twisted her hand in the air. She seemed to grab something and hold it in her hand, and then she threw it to the ground, right in front of the charred and broken tree stump where the Source had been.

Nothing left her hand, there was nothing to see—but the tree stump split with a huge *crack!* as if cleaved by a giant maul, and the ground groaned under their feet like an earthquake, almost shaking everyone off their feet. Then water erupted from the ground.

It bubbled up through the split tree and welled over, spilling onto the leaves. The earth continued to split beneath it, an actual crack in the ground, growing bigger and bigger, and the water filled it. Within a moment, right in front of their eyes, Melita had reopened the Source.

I felt like I'd been hit with a baseball bat, and it had permanently reduced my brain to mush. So much had just happened right in front of me, and I couldn't understand any of it. But somehow I knew that Melita had thrown magick at the ground and made the Source appear after all this time, after all Daedalus's effort.

"That was Daedalus's power," Melita said, then turned to Thais, who looked just as pole-struck as I felt. "You never let power that big or that dark loose into the world, *cher*. Someone dark might find it, might use it to reopen a magickal well that would only make her stronger. Poor Daedalus. But it saved me from performing a difficult and time-consuming spell."

On the ground, Daedalus lay unmoving. I hoped he wasn't dead. I couldn't believe Thais had really done it, stripped his powers from him. She must have been planning this, this whole time, and she'd never told me.

And now I had the horrible knowledge that *he* was my ancestor. I hadn't minded learning from him, but to know I was related to him, however distantly long ago, was sickening.

Of course, if it were Daedalus who'd fathered the baby and not Richard . . . But no, I couldn't even begin to think about all of that right now.

I saw Nan start to edge her way closer to me. The earth had literally split open, and the crack was widening and filling rapidly with water. It was maybe eight feet across now, twelve feet long, and who knew how deep. Melita had rent the actual earth, and I knew that I would never see magick that big or strong or dark again.

Melita had said that Thais and I were dark, as evil as she was. I prayed that wasn't true. But I'd just seen my sister strip a powerful witch of his powers, practically killing him. He'd been writhing in pain, clearly tortured and anguished, and she had kept on. I don't think I could have done it. But she was my identical twin. If she had darkness in her, maybe even more darkness than light, then so must I.

But she was still my sister, and she looked as awful as I did, horrified and sick and ashamed. I went to her, putting my arm around her shoulders, just as Nan came up to us.

"Are you both all right?" she asked again.

I just laughed, a brittle, choking sound.

"No, they're not all right." A new voice coming from the woods made us all start.

I saw Manon, the new, older Manon walking toward us, her fists clenched, and remembered that Daedalus had asked some of the Treize to meet us

230

here at dawn. Dawn had come and gone, and I'd barely noticed.

"Manon—you look . . . different," said Melita.

"You don't," Manon said shortly. "I wish you'd never come back. The twins aren't all right," she repeated. "They'll never be all right. I don't want a full Treize, I don't want the Source, I don't want there to ever be another rite. I am finally something close to normal." She gestured to herself, no longer a child, almost a woman.

"But Daedalus—" Nan began as Manon raised her hand.

"Manon, don't be stu—" Melita began, but Manon cried out words that sent a chill down my spine and threw something at us. A rock? It glinted in the sun—a crystal? Melita shouted over her, but the crystal hit me and Thais where our shoulders were pressed together, and before I blinked again, I realized I was frozen, completely bound in a way I'd never been.

Thais

My eyes slanted to Clio, and she wore the same wide-eyed look of fear I was sure was on my face. I tried to move but felt like I was encased in ice. This must be how Daedalus felt. Panicking, I realized that the Source had widened and was practically under our feet. I looked for Petra and saw that she was reaching out for us, but everything was moving in slow motion. Her mouth opened, but her words were incomprehensible. Her hands grabbed at us but never reached us.

The ground beneath my feet gave way and I felt the rushing coldness of the Source lapping at my ankle. Then it was under our feet. I screamed, but no words came out.

Then we were falling, stuck together, eyes wide, the earth beneath us splitting wider to take us in. The cold water was shocking, and I was stunned that we were sinking in the Source, the water sucking us under.

This is how my darkness ends. As the water closed over our heads, an unexpected calmness came over me. It was over—it was all over. Somehow, it suddenly made sense. Starting with my dad's death, everything in my life had been building up to this moment. Something bad had happened to me and brought my own darkness to the surface, as Melita had said. And now it was ending with my death. It seemed appropriate, after what I had done to Daedalus, after the revelation of what I might do in the future.

These thoughts passed through my brain in an instant as I stared into my sister's eyes. We were in the Source, and instead of giving us life, it was going to bring us death. Melita had just opened this split, but we'd already sunk out of sight of the surface into water that was becoming colder and darker with each passing second.

We couldn't move. Our eyes open wide, we could only stare at each other, unable to speak or struggle in any way. Manon had killed us to prevent another rite from ever taking place. With me and Clio dead, they wouldn't have a full Treize ever again—not only would we not be there, but we'd never have children to continue Cerise's line. And Manon would . . . what? Keep aging? Grow old and die?

Clio's hand tightened on mine—we could do that at least. I was a good swimmer. Daddy had taught me. But I was frozen like a block of ice and couldn't kick my way to the surface. All I could do was hold my twin's hand and watch her drown.

How much time had passed? We were both still holding our breath.

I was going to die today, right now.

It was incomprehensible. I understood it but couldn't wrap my mind around the idea.

The water was dark but clear. I could barely make out Clio's face. I'd gone seventeen years without knowing she existed, my other half, my identical twin. I'd known her barely more than two months, but I was about to lose her forever. And she would lose me.

I thought about Luc, and my heart twisted. Clio was the other half of *me*, but Luc was the other half of my soul. I knew my death would hurt him. And it would hurt Petra too, but not nearly as much as Clio's death would. Petra would be devastated by Clio's death. I would miss her. But I would be seeing my dad soon. I hoped. Frowning, I wondered what the *bonne magie* had to say about the afterlife. I didn't know! There was so much I didn't know.

A look of pain crossed Clio's face, and then a stream of air bubbles escaped her lips. My eyes opened wider, and I saw she looked panicked. I clutched her hand tighter, though the water was so cold my fingers were getting numb.

No, Clio, don't give up, not yet. I tried to send her thoughts, but I couldn't tell if she could feel them.

She coughed soundlessly, and I dimly saw her mouth open as she inhaled water. *No, Clio, stop, stop! Hold your breath!* This was it. She was drowning! *God, Clio, please don't leave me!* My chest felt like a mule had kicked it, and my ears were about to burst, but I hadn't given up.

Inches away, Clio met my eyes one last time, and she smiled slightly. *I love you,* her mouth formed, and no air bubbles came out. Her fingers tightened a tiny bit on mine, then her eyes, identical to mine, drifted shut. I felt her body go limp.

I held on to her hand as hard as I could.

My twin was dead. Now it was just me again.

And it was my turn to die.

Should I repent of everything? Dad and I hadn't gone to church much—I didn't know what I was supposed to do. Ask for forgiveness? Part of me could never be sorry for what I'd done to Daedalus.

I'd spent my whole life obeying rules, following directions, trying to do what was right, but I didn't know the rules about dying. I didn't know how to do it.

I guess I should close my eyes. . . .

Not Part of the Plan at All

Petra lunged toward Manon, who was leaning over the Source, a satisfied look on her face. She pushed Manon's shoulders as hard as she could, which in her weakened state meant that she barely budged her.

"Stop! Stop! Are you crazy?" Petra said hoarsely. Bracing her feet on the ground, she knelt by the water, trying to grab the twins. They were out of reach already, sinking like two flawed, beautiful stones to the earth's core. "Help me, someone!" she cried. Daedalus was useless, barely alive, but the others were supposed to be here! Daedalus had asked Ouida to come this morning with a few others, and Ouida had told Petra and the rest of the uninvited.

Manon was snatching at Petra's shirt, trying to pull her away from the Source. "They're gone! I'm sorry, but they're gone!" she cried.

Vaguely Petra heard voices, but she was trying to hold off Manon and couldn't look.

"Melita! Melita, no!" Jules's voice overlaid Melita's, and Petra realized her daughter's voice was shouting a death spell. Aghast, she turned in time to see Melita fling a hand at . . . Manon. Manon stiffened, her head tossed back, eyes open in surprise, and then she crumpled. Petra caught her as she fell, and she was dead. Actually dead, after all this time. Days after she'd finally wanted to live. Her face was more beautiful than it had been when she'd looked like a child. Her eyes were open, the color of the sky on a clear night.

"Manon!" Sophie shrieked, running forward.

A death spell? Manon could die from a death spell? But others of them had tried it before—it had never worked. Nothing had worked. But now Manon was dead. Petra was beyond grief, beyond tears. Manon had killed the twins, and her own daughter had proven herself a murderer—again.

The cloudy skies opened up then, as if to cry for her, and a chilling rain began to fall. Then Sophie was dropping onto the wet leaves next to her, and Luc was shouting something, and Ouida was crouched over Daedalus.

"How could she die?" Sophie said wonderingly.

"Where are the twins?" Richard said, grabbing Petra's shoulder. "Where are they?"

"Thais!" Luc shouted. "Thais! Where are you?" He wheeled to face Melita. "If you've done them harm, I swear by the goddess I will hunt you down."

"Luc! They're in the Source!" Petra pointed at the deep fissure in the ground, barely registering the horror and anger on his face.

"Sophie, Sophie—I'm sorry." Marcel's voice was

237

quiet as he knelt next to where she was sobbing over Manon's body. He put his arm around her shaking shoulders.

"Move, move!" Melita said, pushing him out of the way. Petra watched, numb, as Melita closed her eyes and began an incantation that Petra immediately recognized as dark and ancient. The surface of the Source began to roil. Petra stared at it uncomprehendingly as Claire and Jules came and helped her up.

"*Pauvre petite*," Jules said, looking down at Manon, but Petra was transfixed by the clear water, bubbling over the edges of the hole. She stood unsteadily, holding Claire's hand, and felt like she was a thousand years old.

Melita kept speaking, words Petra had never heard, and then, shimmering in the water, getting closer to the surface, she saw the white skin of the twins' faces.

"Clio! Thais!" Dropping again, she lunged for the water and felt the silken swirl of soft black hair. The girls' faces bobbed above the surface, but their eyes were shut, their faces still. "Help me!" Petra cried.

Together she, Ouida, Richard, Luc, and Jules pulled the twins' bodies from the Source. As soon as Petra touched them, she knew: one was dead, one was alive.

"Clio!" Richard said, his face ashen. Roughly pushing Petra aside, he scooped up Clio's dripping body and cradled her on his lap, wiping wet, black hair off her beautiful, tranquil face. He rocked

238

slightly back and forth, smoothing her hair, her face, her skin under his fingers. His face was a mask of pain. "Clio, Clio, Clio," he whispered.

Petra thought dimly, *Richard?*

A few feet away, Luc had turned Thais on her side and slammed his palm against her back again and again. Waiting through a lifetime of slow seconds, Petra thought she was imagining things when Thais coughed, water running out of her mouth.

"Thais, Thais," Luc murmured, holding her, rubbing her back. Thais gagged and choked, coughing and then sucking in breath. She was alive. Petra had lost one and kept one.

"Actually, I need them both," Melita said quietly. Furious, Richard tried to block her, but Melita dropped like a bird of prey and struck her fist hard against Clio's chest. The few words she spit out sounded as if they had come straight from hell. Except that Petra knew none of them believed in hell.

Richard stared, and before Petra's eyes Clio's white face seemed to color again. Melita could give life as well as take it away.

Thais

I was sleeping, and the next thing I knew, I was coughing up water and gagging while someone pounded my back too hard.

Blinking groggily, I realized I was on wet leaves on the ground, and it was raining, and the only part of me that was warm was the hand on my back. I looked around. Petra sat a few feet away, her face tragic, almost skeletal. Luc hovered over me. It was his hand on my back. I'd thought I'd never see him again. Now, realizing I was still alive and he was here, I started crying but tried to sit up.

"Where's Clio? Where's my sister?" She'd died in front of me—I'd seen it, felt it.

"Shh, shh," Luc said, smoothing my sodden hair.

"*Where's Clio?*" I said, my voice a croak.

"Here."

I turned to see Richard looking down at Clio, transfixed, and I thought, *I was right. He loves her.*

And she was dead.

Except she was blinking.

Blinking? I sat up.

My sister was alive.

Clio

Is there a white light, a tunnel, people who have passed before holding out their hands?

Maybe. I'm not going to spoil the surprise.

Richard was holding me, stroking my hair. Thais was alive. Petra was alive.

Every member of the Treize was there: Claire and Jules, holding hands. Sophie, weeping over Manon's body. Ouida, kneeling next to Daedalus. Marcel, sitting next to Sophie. Axelle, who had arrived and was sitting on Daedalus's other side, looking amazingly torn up over his broken condition.

And Luc, who had chosen Thais, not me.

Richard held me tensely, seeing me look at Thais and Luc. I looked back at him, into his dark eyes that showed every emotion I'd never thought he had: fear, hope, love—you name it, I saw it there in his tears.

"I'm glad to see you," I whispered, and reached up to touch his face.

Beginning Again

Richard paused before he rang the doorbell at Petra's house. Inside he felt Petra, Ouida, and Luc, and he grimaced. Well, might as well get it over with. He rang the doorbell.

This morning felt like a hundred years ago. He'd seen Clio dead, wearing her necklace of water, just like Cerise had 242 years ago. There was still a lingering pain over Cerise; there always would be. He was both sad and relieved to know that he hadn't fathered her baby. The idea that she'd been with Daedalus even once disgusted him—he really hadn't known Cerise, had he?

What he felt for Clio was a thousand times deeper, stronger. Scarier.

Ouida answered the door. Examining his face, she hugged him silently. He hugged her back, relaxing into her embrace for the first time.

"How's Petra?"

"Surprisingly good, considering everything," she said.

In the kitchen, the kettle was whistling. Luc and

Petra sat there, and Ouida was right—Petra didn't look nearly as bad as he'd feared.

"Richard." Petra looked at him, and he saw acceptance in her eyes. "I'm so glad you're all right. What a day. Poor Manon. And Melita—"

"Is gone again," said Ouida.

"Girls okay?" Richard said.

"Thais is upstairs," Luc said, sounding pompous and possessive.

"They're fine, thanks to everyone," said Petra, sipping a steaming cup of something herby and medicinal.

"How the hell could Melita kill Manon?" Richard asked bluntly.

Petra's face twisted in pain. "I think—I just think Melita is still the strongest of us all. As strong as she made us, she kept the most power for herself."

"Was she the one who was trying to kill the twins?" Richard's face flushed. "I mean, after me," he mumbled.

"If she was, they'd have been dead," Ouida said. "No—actually, we still don't know who it was. Maybe Daedalus? He's not coherent enough to ask. We just don't know."

Richard stayed standing, casting a curt glance at Luc. "I want to see Clio." He looked at Petra as if daring her to try to stop him.

"She's upstairs," Petra said. "I don't know if she's awake or not."

Richard nodded, then turned and started up the stairs. He had no idea what he'd find. He braced himself for the cool, disdainful Clio to be firmly

243

back in place, death experience notwithstanding. Well, he would just start over. He had time.

At the top of the stairs, one door was shut, and one was slightly open. Thais was behind the closed door, Richard sensed, and crossed the landing. He tapped gently on the open door, mostly as a formality, then pushed it open and immediately shut it behind him.

Clio was propped up in her bed, not reading or doing anything, just looking at the ceiling. She seemed startled to see him, especially here, in her bedroom, and he was surprised she hadn't felt him come up the stairs.

He stopped a few feet from her bed, taking in her scrapes and bruises, her still-pale face. She was wearing some unsexy kind of flannel something with pictures of sushi all over it. He had no idea what to say so instead looked at her challengingly, hoping to start an argument at least, because it would be some kind of interaction.

Her slanted, leaf green eyes looked at him, and then . . . she held out her hand.

Taken aback, Richard didn't move for a moment, then stepped forward and took it. Amazingly, she shifted on her narrow bed, making room for him. After a tiny hesitation, he sat down next to her, his heart pounding. She leaned against him, putting one arm over his chest, and his throat closed up.

He held her to him, stroking her hair, thinking about how he'd almost lost her forever.

"I guess it's all over," she said, her voice still raspy and weak.

He sighed and kissed her forehead. "It's never over, baby."

Clio seemed to accept this. She looked up at him with her beautiful, cat-shaped eyes, the rose-colored birthmark of a fleur-de-lis on her left cheek.

"Just hold me, okay?"

He nodded, and they snuggled closer together. It began to rain outside, the drops hitting the window-panes. But in here they were warm and dry and safe. At least for now.

Thais

What was left of the Treize had gathered and built the magickal equivalent of Fort Knox around us in protection spells. I knew Petra was still worried that they didn't know who'd tried to hurt us, but with Melita gone and no chance of a rite happening, I felt safe enough to venture out of Petra's house. My house. My family's house.

It was a beautiful fall day, which everyone had told me was very rare for New Orleans. It was chilly and clear, and the air was almost crisp. I'd decided to take a walk up on the levee, by the river, which was only three blocks from our street. A shell road topped the levee all the way up to Baton Rouge, and people rode bikes and horses along here all the time.

Now I walked along, watching the endless river with its traffic of barges and steamboats.

Clio seemed happy with Richard, and the two of them suited each other better than I would have guessed. I was happy for her, having seen glimpses of the old, fun Clio peeking out in the last couple of days.

As for me, I was alive, and I had a family and a home. I was fine.

Sighing, I left the shell road and went down the levee a bit to sit on the warm, soft grass there and watch the water. I'd sat on the levee another time, a lifetime ago, where the river ran next to the Quarter. Now I turned my face to the sky, closing my eyes, enjoying the sun on my skin.

I sat like that for minutes, not thinking, just letting myself be, aware of all the ways I was connected to the world, all the things I felt now, life and magick and beauty.

"Thais."

I jumped—I'd come to rely on being able to sense people around me. Hearing a voice at my back without sensing someone coming was really startling.

Especially considering who it was.

Luc sat down next to me, a Greek god once again, the sunlight glinting off his perfect, chiseled profile.

"You look better," he said, appraising me.

"So do you," I replied.

He laughed dryly and touched his cheek with one hand, as if to make sure he hadn't uglified again. He was wearing worn jeans and a soft button-down shirt under a leather jacket, and he looked . . . beautiful.

"Thais," he said, taking a breath. "When you and Clio realized that I'd betrayed you, I thought I'd lost you forever."

My face stiffened, and I looked away. He was only inches from me, and I felt the heat of his knee reaching mine.

"Then, when I did this to myself at the rite, I was really sure that I'd lost you forever." He gestured at his face, and I glanced up, startled. He nodded. "At the rite I asked for the chance to make you love me again. That face was what the spell produced. It was meant to knock the wind out of my sails and figure out who I was inside. To help me understand what was important, what I really cared about, about myself and my life."

I didn't know what to say.

He let out a deep breath. "Then, three days ago, when we hauled you and Clio out of the Source, and I saw you . . ." He looked away, plucking at the grass with nervous fingers. When he spoke again, it was barely a whisper. "Then I knew what losing you would really feel like." His dark blue eyes met mine, and somehow I understood that he was different— that he wasn't trying to win me, wasn't asking anything of me.

"And I wanted to say—everything seems all right since you're alive." He cleared his throat and looked out at the river. "I don't care how I look or where I live. I don't care if you learn magick or not or stay with Petra and Clio. It doesn't matter if you don't love me, it doesn't matter if you love someone else—whatever makes you happy. As long as you're alive in this world, then everything is all right. And I want to be alive too. As long as

248

you are. That's the only thing of real value to me."

I couldn't speak for a moment. "Melita said—I'm as dark she is. It's in my line, inescapable. I stripped Daedalus of his powers. Only someone . . . awful could do something like that." I looked down at my scuffed clogs, picked at a hole in my cords.

Luc didn't say anything, and finally I looked up at him.

"Darkness is in everyone, Thais," he said gently. He reached across and took one of my chilled hands in his. "In me, in you, in Petra and Ouida and everyone. And so is light. Darkness is a choice, a path. Every day we all have to make the choice to choose good, choose light. We make the choice against darkness, against evil, every day, a thousand times a day, our whole lives."

"I'm afraid I don't have choices," I said, my words barely a whisper. This was my deepest fear, and it was devastating to say it out loud.

Luc leaned over and kissed my hair. I didn't flinch away from him.

"I promise you, you do," he said firmly. "Even Melita has choices. Everyone always does. I believe that from now on, you'll make the best choices you can." He laced his fingers with mine, and it felt so incredibly comforting, so incredibly perfect.

"Thais," he said, sounding very unsure. "I would . . . be grateful . . . if you would choose . . . somehow . . . ." He cleared his throat again. "To be my friend."

I could hardly hear the last words. I looked

down at our fingers, his long tan ones, my smaller, paler ones, and I knew that I wanted to hold his hand forever.

"Yes," I said, and in that moment, the burden of my dark inheritance seemed to lighten a hundred-fold. "Yes, Luc. I'll be your . . . friend."